IN COLD DAYLIGHT

PAULINE ROWSON

Fathom

IN COLD DAYLIGHT
First published in 2006 by Fathom
Reprinted in 2008

65 Rogers Mead
Hayling Island
Hampshire
England
PO11 0PL

ISBN: 9780955098215

Printed in Great Britain by J. H. Haynes & Co. Ltd., Sparkford

Fathom is an imprint of Rowmark Limited

PAULINE ROWSON

Pauline Rowson was raised in Portsmouth, the setting for her crime novels. For many years she ran her own marketing and public relations agency and is now a writer and a professional conference speaker. She is the author of several marketing, self-help and motivational books. She lives in Hampshire and can never be far from the sea for any length of time without suffering withdrawal symptoms.

For Chrissy and my mum

For fire fighters everywhere – the true heroes –
and especially for Bob and Red Watch, Southsea

AUTHOR'S NOTE

This novel is set primarily in Portsmouth, Hampshire, on the south coast of England. Residents and visitors of Portsmouth must forgive the author for using her imagination and poetic licence in changing the names of places, streets and locations. This novel is entirely a work of fiction. The names, characters, businesses, locations and incidents portrayed in it are entirely the work of the author's imagination. Any resemblance to actual persons, living or dead, events or locations is entirely coincidental.

PROLOGUE

If it hadn't been for the break-in on the day of the funeral I might never have got involved. But that and Jack's note urging me to take care of his wife, Rosie, obliged me. I had let him down in life; I wasn't about to let him down in death.

Danger wasn't usually my kind of thing, though. I was just happy to let things be. But the past has a nasty habit of catching up with you and mine had done just that. As I stood around Jack's grave in the bleak Portsmouth cemetery in December the memory of another funeral fifteen years ago had rushed in and almost suffocated me.

I tried to shut out the image but I couldn't. Some things never went away. They just lay in wait for you. I wanted to leave but knew I couldn't.

I had closed my eyes and tried to block out the past but it refused to go. I knew then that it wouldn't. I had run away once. This time I had a feeling that running away wouldn't be an option.

CHAPTER 1

I woke with the mother of all hangovers. I could hear my wife Faye moving about the house. I groaned and reached for the clock only to find my arm waving in thin air. I peeled open my eyes. The electric light stabbed at me like a laser beam. Of course I was in the lounge. It was the day after Jack's funeral. I hadn't been able to sleep. My mouth felt like sandpaper; my tongue two sizes too big for me.

What on earth was Faye doing? She sounded as if she was trying to break the record for the

number of times she could circumnavigate the
house wearing hobnailed boots whilst spinning
crockery. I guessed she was punishing me for
going to Rosie's aid last night, but what was I
supposed to do? Rosie had only just buried her
husband, and to return home from the wake to
find her house ransacked... I couldn't leave her
to face that alone. And I couldn't let Jack down.
'Look after Rosie for me, Adam'. The words on Jack's
last message to me obliged me, but I would have
gone anyway.

I wasn't usually in favour of corporal
punishment; last night had changed my mind. I
thought hanging was too good for the burglars.
The odd thing was though, nothing had been
taken, or so Rosie's daughter, Sarah, had said after
a quick check round. Rosie's jewellery was still
in her bedroom and even I could see, through
the chaos of strewn condolence cards and
flowers, that the TV and hi fi were in the lounge,
and intact. I'd only glimpsed Jack's study but it
was enough for me to notice that the computer
had been smashed but not the printer. Why that
and nothing else? It didn't make any sense, but
then neither did Jack's death.

Sarah had taken her mother back to her flat

whilst I had stayed behind to talk to the police and arrange for the locksmith to change the busted front door lock. It was the least I could do.

'You're awake then.' Faye's reproachful tone was like barbed wire in my brain.

I opened my eyes again and grunted. Faye was looking at me as if I was something the cat had sicked up on the carpet. Remembering our row last night I wasn't surprised. Faye had wanted me to take her out to celebrate winning her first new client account since her promotion to account director at the London advertising agency where she worked. Instead I had dumped her for Jack's widow. I tried smiling but that must have made me look worse because she tutted and tossed her blonde hair.

'How much did you drink last night, Adam?'

I watched her pick up the television remote control and put it beside the television set. Faye always liked things in their proper place and I wasn't where I should have been. I thought if she could pick me up and tidy me away she'd be happy. Her pretty face was frowning as she lifted the almost empty whisky bottle with thumb and forefinger. I felt a stab of guilt as she carried it as through to the kitchen as if it were contaminated.

'Does it matter?' I heaved myself up on one arm.

'Of course it matters. I don't wish to be married to a drunk.'

She returned from the kitchen and stared down at me, her hands on her slender hips. She was dressed for work in a smart black trouser suit.

'What time is it?' I asked.

'Time you did some work. You can't mourn forever. Jack wouldn't want you to.'

Since Rosie had telephoned me to say that Jack was dead I hadn't been able to lift a paintbrush. That was twelve days ago. I was beginning to wonder if I would ever paint again.

'You'll miss your train,' I grunted, standing up and making a valiant attempt not to stagger. The expression on her face told me I'd said the wrong thing.

'I'm taking the car to London and I'm staying in the agency flat until Friday. In case you haven't noticed Christmas is less than three weeks away and I've got a great deal to do.'

'When did you decide this?' I asked surprised, stumbling into the kitchen and almost tripping over Boudicca who give a loud meow and glared at me. Not you too, I thought, flicking on the kettle. I turned to face Faye then wished I hadn't as the movement caused my head to spin.

'Last night, after you rushed out. I called Stewart. He said it was OK.'

Was this my punishment for going to the aid of my best friend's widow? I'd never met Faye's boss, but I didn't much care for him, probably because I was sick of hearing about him.

She continued, 'I thought it would give you time to do some work and prepare for the exhibition on Saturday. I've gone to a great deal of trouble to get a top London gallery owner down for it, not to mention the Lord Mayor of Portsmouth and our MP.'

'I know. I haven't forgotten,' I only wished I could. Faye was determined to make me into a household name. Me? I wouldn't even have bothered to have an exhibition. Or if I had to, I would have preferred to absent myself. I find showing off my work excruciatingly embarrassing. A decided drawback for an artist.

I reached for a mug and spooned in some coffee. I opened my mouth to talk about Rosie but Faye got there first.

'Are you even going to try and paint today?'

Faye eyed me with contempt.

'You'll miss your car.' Further discussion was pointless.

She snatched up her briefcase and car keys, glared at me and stomped out. 'And that is that,' I said to the cat who lifted her head as if to say what did you expect, then turned tail on me and hopped through the cat flap.

I drank my coffee slumped on the sofa. I'm not very good at arguing. Giving in is more my speciality. Faye was understandably peeved that I had deserted her in her hour of glory. Perhaps I should call her and apologise? I hate an atmosphere. Maybe later.

I closed my eyes but couldn't blot out the events of the previous night. The police had said drug addicts were probably to blame for the break-in, but what sort of drug addicts would leave jewellery and other items that could have been sold for a quick buck? I had voiced my opinion to the younger, stouter police officer. He'd said, 'If they're drugged up, sir, who knows what is going through their mind.' I thought his reply a cop-out but then he didn't know about my last conversation with Jack.

'I'm being followed,' Jack had said when I had

telephoned him two weeks ago. I had laughed and told him he was being paranoid.

'Why would anyone want to follow you?' I had teased.

'I can't tell you yet, Adam, it's too dangerous, but I'm almost there.'

'Where?'

'At the truth, give me a few more days.'

Only Jack hadn't had a few more days. The day after he had entered a derelict burning building. It was his job putting out fires. It could have happened to any fire fighter. But it hadn't. It had happened to Jack. I wasn't laughing now.

I poured the remainder of my coffee down the sink staring out across the windswept garden to the rising slopes of Portsdown Hill. Two forlorn-looking ponies shivered in the cold. Jack wasn't given to hallucinations. If he said someone was following him then they were, but who and why? What was he doing that was dangerous? And why send me the postcard? I wasn't going to get the answers by staring out of windows.

I threw on some old clothes and trekked across the garden to my studio. The smattering of snow that had covered that hummock of earth in the bleak cemetery yesterday had vanished overnight leaving in its wake a chill grey day, damp and miserable.

I gazed at the canvasses of seascapes hating them all, seeing nothing but mediocrity before my eyes travelled to Jack's postcard. I had only received it yesterday even though it had been posted the day Jack had died. I guessed it had got caught up in the Christmas mail. It had been a shock seeing his handwriting, and a puzzle as to why he had written it and what he had written. I didn't need to read it again because every word was etched on my mind but I unpinned it and turned over the picture of Turner's 'The Fighting Temeraire'.

Look after 'Rosie' for me, Adam. You're an accomplished artist and a good friend. Happy Sailing!
Best Jack
4 July 1994

Why date it July when he had sent it in December? Why put the year as 1994 when it was 2006? And why had he underlined certain letters? S I E D N G O. It was some sort of code. I wasn't good at word puzzles like Jack had been. The only words that leapt out at me were DIES,

ENDS and GOD. It was as if Jack knew he was going to die. But that was ridiculous; how could he have known that a gas cylinder would explode the moment he rushed in?

I recalled my conversation with Steve Langton, at the wake. He was a friend and a DI at the city police station. I hadn't told him about the postcard or my last conversation with Jack.

'Any more news on the fire?' I had asked him.

'Nothing. We've questioned the local kids and carried out a house to house but you know that area, they'd rather shield a murderer than co-operate with the police.'

'Do you think it was intentional?'

'You mean that gas cylinder placed inside deliberately and the building flashed up? It looks like it to me and to fire investigations; they found traces of an accelerant. Whether it was kids larking around or some nutter who gets his sexual jollies from setting fire to things and then watching big red fire engines turn up I don't know. But we're still on the case; I'll get to the truth.'

And there was that word again: truth. What was the truth? And had kids or a nutcase really caused Jack's death? Could someone have planted that gas cylinder knowing that Jack would be the first to enter that burning building? If so, how? There was only one way to find out and that was to ask Jack's colleagues. I hadn't liked to yesterday, since the wake was hardly the appropriate place, but this morning was different.

I climbed on my motorbike and headed down into the city, diverting to Rosie's on the way. If I could just get into Jack's study I might find something that could give me some idea of what he had been doing. I was disappointed to find no one in but not surprised. I was about to leave when a window screeched open to my right.

'Can I help?'

I craned my neck to the first floor bay window of the house next door. A woman with short spiky brown hair was eyeing me curiously.

I was about to politely refuse when I had second thoughts. 'You might be able to.'

'Hang on. I'll come down.'

She was in her early thirties and dressed scruffily in faded jeans and a T-shirt that Faye wouldn't even have done the housework in. I hadn't seen her at the funeral. I would have remembered those olive-green eyes and that elfin face.

'I'm Adam Greene, a friend of Rosie's,' I introduced myself.

'How is she? I must call round.'

'She's at her daughter's, but she'll be back later. Did you hear about the break-in, yesterday?'

'No! How awful. The bastards.'

'My sentiments exactly. I was wondering if you saw or heard anything suspicious between three and seven o'clock.'

'No. I had an appointment in London, which was why I couldn't make the funeral. I can ask my landlady, Sharon. I'm only the lodger: Jody Piers.'

'If she remembers anything perhaps you'd ask her to give me a call.' I handed her my card.

'Marine artist,' she said, studying it. 'We have something in common. I'm a marine biologist.'

My eyes connected with hers for a fleeting moment. I liked what I saw. I liked even more how I felt before I told myself that I was married.

She said, 'Shouldn't the police be doing this, asking questions?'

I pulled myself together and said, 'They probably will.' I saw her sceptical look. It made me smile.

'Was Jack your friend?'

'Yes.'

'You must be feeling like shit.'

That was putting it mildly. A woman I didn't know had summed up my emotions more completely than my wife.

I had trouble getting those olive-green eyes out of my mind as I weaved my way through the heavy pre-Christmas traffic to the fire station. I didn't mind. They were nice eyes and they helped to replace that picture of Jack's coffin. *But not Jack or my feelings of guilt.* Why hadn't I seen more of him over the last couple of months? I might then have discovered what the devil he'd been up to. But I'd been too intent on finishing off the paintings for the exhibition. I cursed myself, and Faye, for that. Jack was one of the most laid back men I had ever known and yet his voice had sounded urgent and troubled in that last conversation. And I'd ignored it.

I was told that Red Watch weren't on duty again until Friday, three days away. Damn. I would have to wait until then because I didn't know any of them personally apart from Des Brookfield who had come sailing with us a few times in the past before buying his own boat. He was no longer on the watch but stationed at headquarters. I had

never really liked him. He was too flash, too
ambitious, too everything for me. He had been
at the funeral looking important in his uniform,
a distraught expression on his swarthy features.
Of course he was upset, I told myself, but with
Brookfield it always looked like an act rather than
the genuine article. I was probably doing him a
disservice. Anyway he would hardly know what
Jack had been doing. There seemed little I could
do until Friday unless Rosie returned home soon
and I could ask her. She might know.

I swung into one of the parking bays along the
seafront, as far away from the fun fair as I could
get and pulled off my helmet. As I sniffed the
salt air and stared across the grey turbulent sea
to the Isle of Wight, Jack's words came back to
me: 'Listen to the sea, Adam. She has all the
answers.' Answers to what, I thought, when I
hardly knew the questions!

Jack's message flashed into my mind: *Happy
Sailing!* A reference, I guessed, to the fact that in
October I had bought his yacht. How could I be
happy sailing her now when every moment
aboard would remind me of those happier times
with Jack: the laughs and the drinks, the serious
conversations and the companionable silences.

God, I would miss him. *Just as I had missed Alison*. I tensed. I had tried to forget her. I thought I had succeeded until yesterday when Jack's funeral had pulled me back. Now I knew the memory of my former girlfriend – though that word hardly expressed how much she'd meant to me – would never leave me. Nor would that of her violent and unexpected death. I had come to Portsmouth twelve years ago to forget. It wasn't far enough. Nowhere ever would be.

I didn't want to think of her. Jack. Think of Jack. But somehow I knew Alison would continue to intrude on my thoughts. She wasn't going to go away, just as the puzzle over Jack's death wasn't going to until I solved it.

Action was what I needed. I started the bike and swung it round as another motorbike drew up a few yards from me. The driver removed his helmet. He looked vaguely familiar but I couldn't place him. I nodded at him but got no response. Perhaps I was mistaken.

I returned home and had another stab at the coded message. I got a further half a dozen words from the letters that Jack had underlined; including SINGED. It wasn't much help.

'What was Jack doing, Boudicca?' I asked the

cat who opened one lazy eye at me as if to say how the devil should I know?

'No, me neither.'

I wondered if I would ever know, but I knew I had to try and find out.

CHAPTER 2

Rosie's sleep-starved face matched my own as she let me in the next morning. She was so thin that I thought she would slip through a crack in the pavement if she stepped outside. She was still in black save for a silver locket.

I followed her through to the lounge and drew up amazed. The condolence cards were back on the mantelshelf and on the book cabinets, some of the flowers had been rescued and new ones filled a couple of vases. The furniture was all in its proper place.

'You've worked very hard,' I said, unzipping my leather jacket and pulling it off.

'Not me, the children and Jody, my neighbour. Everyone's been so kind especially you, Adam. I can't thank you enough for what you did.'

'It was nothing. Jack was a good friend.' My eyes fell on photographs of him around the room. What I wouldn't have given at that moment to hear his voice call out from the bedroom or the kitchen, 'Be there in just a tick, mate, running late.' Jack was always running late except for his death, which was the only time he had ever been early. Too early.

I removed my jacket and put it on the parquet flooring along with my helmet and gloves, then sat down opposite her. All night I'd wrestled with Jack's code to no avail. When I had finally slept I had dreamt of the blessed thing. I was grateful to it though for keeping memories of Alison at bay. My subconscious had performed as miserably as my conscious mind. I still hadn't cracked it. I was counting on Rosie enlightening me, or at least finding something in Jack's study that could point me in the right direction.

'I'm glad you came round, Adam. I didn't get a

chance to speak to you at the wake, and it was hardly the place.'

She knew. She was about to tell me what Jack had meant by that last conversation. She appeared nervous and I wondered what was coming next. I hoped it would be the answer to that code.

'I have to know the truth, Adam, and if Jack confided in anyone it would have been you. Was Jack having an affair?'

I started. That was the last thing I'd expected to hear. And it was utter nonsense. 'Of course he wasn't.'

'Then why was he so moody and secretive? You know that wasn't like him, he was always so cheerful and easy going.'

'It wasn't an affair, Rosie.'

I should tell her about Jack's last conversation with me. I should mention the postcard. But I couldn't. It was obvious to me now that Jack hadn't confided in her and his last message to me was clear in one respect: *Look after Rosie for me*. He didn't want her to know.

'We rowed before he went on shift that night,' she continued. 'I wish we hadn't. I loved him so much…'

I swiftly crossed to her side and lifted her thin

hand in mine. 'Jack loved you.'

It was as if she hadn't heard me. 'He used to spend hours upstairs in his study. He'd lock the door. Why? What was he doing?'

What indeed? Perhaps he'd left something on his computer that could tell me. Then I remembered seeing the computer hard drive smashed. I was beginning to get a very bad feeling about all this and a little voice in my head was saying, back out now while you still can.

Rosie said, 'There were telephone calls too but when I answered, the line would go dead. It has to be another woman. Perhaps she broke in and wrecked the house.'

I doubted it but who did? What on earth could Jack have been doing to warrant such violent action? If I followed in his footsteps would I incur some of the same? I glanced across at his photograph, thanks mate, I silently and cynically uttered and could almost imagine his smile before his expression darkened with worry and the strains of his urgent voice came back to me.

I turned my attention back to Rosie who seemed to have shrunken in on herself. I wanted to wipe that pain from her eyes. Squeezing her hand, I said, 'The police said it was drug addicts.'

'They're wrong then. Her name's Stella Hardway. I heard Jack asking for her on the telephone. He thought I was out. I looked her up in the telephone directory but she's not listed.'

I still couldn't believe it. I'd known Jack for twelve years and in all that time he'd not so much as glanced at another woman. I thought it more likely this Stella had something to do with whatever it was Jack was investigating.

'I was wondering, Adam, if you'd mind taking a look in his study. I can't bear to go in there and I wouldn't let Sarah or John touch it. Only there might be something…'

There might. It was what I had been hoping for and what I had come here to do. 'Of course,' I said eagerly, hoping that Rosie didn't want to come with me.

'I'll get you a coffee, Adam.'

I didn't want one but it gave her something to do and left me in peace to get on with my search.

I picked my way through the debris feeling anger knot my stomach at the sight of so much devastation. It was as if someone had desecrated Jack's life. A lump came to my throat and I struggled to get my emotions under control. Through the window I could see the tall palms and leylandii that Jack had planted at the end of the garden to screen him from his neighbours, which were swaying in a brisk wet wind. There was raised decking, a swirling gravel path and a small conservatory. I could see Jack out there now pottering around watering the plants and cursing the cats.

I took a deep breath and faced the room. It was difficult to know where to start but start I had to. I righted the chair and put the drawers back into the desk before bending down to retrieve some of their contents, but my hand hovered over one of the photographs. Why had the intruder removed each photograph from its frame and then smashed the frames? The books too looked as if they had been thumbed through and tossed on the floor each one lay flat, nearly all facing up. If the intruder had run his hand along the shelves scooping them all up then surely they would be lying in any old heap?

I picked up one of the photographs. Jack was in uniform along with some of his colleagues from Red Watch. They were perched on a specially made eight-seater bicycle. Jack was in the front and the photographer had captured the other seven men, with their heads sticking out, behind him. I turned the photograph over; on the back Jack had written, ' *Red Watch – Charity Cycle Ride 1993'* and the men's names. It had been taken the year before I met him.

My mind went back to that dreary May day in 1994. I had not long arrived from London. I had been sitting in a pub overlooking the harbour hugging my beer and feeling so low that I was contemplating ending it all. My life seemed so pointless after Alison's death.

Again, with her memory, came the tightening of my chest and the tingling in my hands. I gave up trying to push her memory away. It was pointless. Instead I let my mind go back to the first time I had met her. It was at the freshers' fair at Oxford. I had heard her laugh before I'd seen her. Her zest for life after my bleak childhood and adolescence was like the spring after a long cold winter. I had found love. It had ended on a Saturday afternoon in my second year at university when she had fallen from a third floor window to her death.

My hands were trembling slightly as I put the photograph aside and began to sift through the debris, but as I methodically began to match up the discarded contents of the lever arch files with the names on their spines, they became still, my racing heart settled down and Alison faded away.

It was a boring job but I persevered. There were household bills, bank statements and insurances. Finally I realised there was one blank file with no name on the spine and as far as I could see no missing contents. But there had been a label on it matching the others because I felt the spine and it was sticky.

There was a tap on the door and Rosie entered clutching a mug of coffee. Her eyes quickly scanned the devastation and then flickered up to me.

'I didn't know it was this bad, Adam. I shouldn't have asked you.'

'It's fine. I've got nothing else to do.' *Except paint* but that was out of the question.

She left me to it. I picked up the cellotape, scissors and other bits of stationery and put them back into a drawer. Jack's sailing and car magazines I replaced in the magazine holders. Then I tackled the books one by one, flicking through them and replacing them on the shelves. There were several novels by Reginald Hill and Robert Goddard; a handful of sporting biographies, a small Bible presented to Jack as a young boy, along with two adventure books he'd won as prizes at school, a few travel books and some old editions of comic books.

I retrieved the smashed photograph frames, carefully lifting them so as not to cut myself on the broken glass, and laid them out on the desk with the photographs on top of them. There were photographs of Jack in the Navy before he joined the Fire Service; Jack in the football team at school aged eleven and Jack in the local cricket team. But there was one missing. I counted eight photograph frames but only seven photographs. I looked again but couldn't find it. Perhaps like the blank lever arch file there had been an empty frame to begin with. But as I closed the door behind me they weren't the only things missing: where were Jack's back-up disks and his diary?

Rosie looked up as I entered the kitchen. 'Did you find anything?'

I knew she was referring to Stella Hardway. I shook my head. It was what I hadn't found that worried me. I spread the photographs out on the kitchen work surface. 'Do you know if any of Jack's framed photos are missing? These are all I could find.'

She glanced down at them and her eyes filled

with tears. 'I'm not sure. I can't remember exactly what he had on his walls. Silly, isn't it, I should remember.'

'Don't worry. It's not important.' I quickly gathered them up. Then I held up the cycle ride photograph. 'Do you think I could keep this one?'

She took it from me with a forlorn expression. 'I remember the day this was taken. There have been so many changes on that watch since then. There's only Brian left now and he almost got killed with Jack. Des Brookfield is a divisional officer at headquarters, Sam Frensham has a hotel in the Cotswolds and Dave Caton lives in France.' As she spoke she pointed to the men in the photograph. 'I'm not sure about Sandy Ditton; I didn't really know him that well or young Scott Burnham who was only on the watch a short time before he died of cancer. Now I come to think of it, Tony and Duggie also died of cancer. No, you keep it, Adam.' She thrust it back at me. 'I've got plenty of other photographs to remind me of Jack. Not that I need them, he's so much a part of me.'

'I couldn't find Jack's computer back-up disks. Do you know where he kept them?' I asked

casually as I smiled my thanks. My heart was
beating a little faster as I waited for her answer.
Was she about to confirm my belief that the
intruder's real intention had been to remove any
evidence of Jack's investigation, whatever that
was, and the destruction created because of his
frantic search of the house?

'In his study, I thought.' She looked surprised.

'You haven't got a safe?'

'No.'

'Would he have given them to Sarah or John?'

'I doubt it, but I can check…'

I forestalled her. 'What about his diary?'

'Isn't that there?' Now she looked puzzled. 'I'll
call Sarah, see if she knows.'

Whilst she was telephoning her daughter, I
poured the remainder of my coffee down the sink
and swilled it round. The kitchen had been
cleaned and tidied since the break-in but I could
still see the red and brown stains on the floor
where the jam and sauces had been ground in
during the break-in. Nothing short of new
flooring would get rid of them.

I could hear the gentle rise and fall of Rosie's
voice while I went on thinking about those
missing items. It all seemed incredible, like

something out of a John Le Carré novel. I told myself for the hundredth time that I must be imagining all this and that there was probably some simple explanation for it.

Rosie returned to tell me that neither Sarah nor John knew anything about disks or Jack's diary. 'I know they weren't in his locker at work.'

'Perhaps he gave them to someone else on the station. I could check.'

'You will tell me if you find out anything about *her*, won't you? Jack might have confided in a colleague. They won't want to tell me for fear of upsetting me, but they might tell you the truth.'

And there was that word again. *'I'm almost there… at the truth.'* Why would Jack say that if it were another woman? Put simply, because it wasn't.

The phone was ringing as I let myself in. I thought it might be Faye.

'Adam, it's Simon.'

I couldn't speak.

'Adam, are you there?'

I thought about putting the phone down, or saying wrong number. It had been fifteen years since I'd seen or spoken to my brother. Why now, I thought, when I had enough to occupy my mind without having to cope with all the emotions that Simon conjured up in me?

'What do you want, Simon?'

'It's Father; he's had a stroke. He's in St Thomas's, London. You'd better come up. How long will it take you to get here?'

'About an hour and a half –'

'I'll meet you in the reception.'

'Simon, I can't…' But the line was already dead.

I replaced the telephone slowly, feeling as if the tide were rushing in at me from all sides leaving me stranded on a rock with no way out. First Alison had returned to haunt me and now a summons from my estranged brother to see the father from whom I had distanced myself for what I had thought was forever. Simon still assumed he could command and I'd simply obey. But then why shouldn't he? He had always got his own way in the past.

I didn't want to go but I knew I had to. There were many times in my life when I wouldn't face my fear but this, I knew, wasn't one of them. This time I had to do it. Damn! Jack's code would have to wait; nevertheless I stuffed his postcard in my pocket.

CHAPTER 3

I made good time. Simon was waiting for me but not in reception. I found him sitting on the edge of one of the beige, vinyl-covered armchairs that lined the small, grey institutionalised room just down the corridor from the Intensive Care Unit. He was leaning forward, his knees apart, hands clasped between them, staring at the floor, his left leg jigging impatiently.

His head came up sharply as I entered and he frowned, but then his expression cleared as recognition dawned. He leapt up and stretched out a hand, with a smile that was perfunctory and condescending.

As I felt the dry, vice-like grip all my memories flooded back: the fair-haired boy eight years my senior, clever, confident, forceful, Father's favourite; the successful son not the one who had failed and so abjectly and publicly.

'He's still unconscious.' Simon moved away, running a hand through his hair. He was going grey at the temples, I noticed. There were no preliminaries; no 'how are you' and 'it's good to see you.' I hadn't really expected them. If we'd been reunited after thirty years instead of fifteen Simon would still have dispensed with the small talk.

'God knows when or even if he'll ever come round,' he continued. 'I'm waiting for the doctor but you know what these places are like, we could be here all night.' He began to pace the room and his presence seemed to take up all the space and air, making me feel insignificant. I wasn't, I told myself, but couldn't believe it. Not here.

Simon had put on weight and had acquired an extra layer of sleekness to go with it. The well-cut and expensive light grey suit fitted him to perfection. His black shoes were polished to within an inch of their life and his jewellery, a wedding ring and Rolex were discreet. He exuded confidence, wealth and power. He wasn't at all what you expected from the traditional image of a scientist. With a first class honours degree in Molecular Science, Simon had followed in Father's footsteps. Next had come a PhD in Biomedical Sciences and then a Member of the Royal Society of Chemistry. Simon had been an expert in DNA technology at a young age, which had made his name in scientific circles and had helped him to build up a substantial biotechnology company and a considerable amount of money if the broadsheets were to be believed.

'Who found him?' I asked, unzipping my leather jacket and pulling it off.

'His housekeeper, this morning.'

'You've been here all day?'

Simon shook his head and frowned at my apparent stupidity. 'Of course not. She discovered him at the bottom of the stairs this morning when she arrived for work and thought at first he'd had a fall, or a heart attack. I didn't get the message until I returned to the laboratory after lunch. I came straight up from Bath. Had to cancel God knows how many meetings.'

Inconvenient, I felt like saying dryly, but sarcasm had been my father's trait not mine. I wondered what I was doing here. I felt no affection for my father. There was too much in my past that I couldn't forgive him for: the hurtful words, the disdainful looks, the sneers, and put downs, the lack of love. But here I was.

Simon said, 'I've spoken to someone who called herself a doctor, looked more like a child on work experience to me. I said I wanted to speak to the consultant or the senior physician at least but that was hours ago, and this is the NHS, so goodness knows when that's likely to be.'

I hoped Simon hadn't made his feelings that plain. It seemed that age hadn't mellowed him, quite the opposite. All the way up here I'd wondered if he would have changed. And Father? If he was conscious and I was to see him, how would he react to me? Would he have changed? I wasn't counting on it, in my experience people rarely did. I sat down, which seemed to goad Simon further.

'I suppose you're just going to wait for

someone to show up,' Simon scoffed. 'I'm not. I've already wasted half a day and I'm damned sure I'm not going to waste a complete evening.'

'Simon…' But he was heading out of the door just as a man with a stethoscope draped around his neck was entering. They almost collided. The doctor stepped back but I was pleased to see he didn't flinch under Simon's hostile glare.

'Mr Greene?'

'Dr Greene,' Simon corrected. 'How is he? What's the prognosis?'

'I'm Dr Newberry, the senior physician in charge of the Intensive Care Unit and looking after your father,' he announced, seemingly unfazed by Simon's domineering behaviour. I warmed to the man. He was in his mid forties, about the same age and height as Simon, but slender and balding, and where Simon looked the picture of affluence and health Dr Newberry looked as if he was on his last pair of trainers and trousers and wouldn't be able to get through the night without falling asleep on the job. Simon refused to sit and loomed over us.

Dr Newberry addressed us both, his eye contact flicking between us. 'Your father is unconscious but he is comfortable. We're arranging for a scan, which will give us a clearer image of the blood flow, and of how much damage there is. Then we will be able to give you a better prognosis.' His voice was gentle but firm. 'If it's any consolation he's not in pain. You can see him if you wish and of course you are welcome to stay as long as you want but there really is very little you can do. If you return tomorrow you should be able to see the consultant who will be in a better position to give you more information.'

'And that's it?' Simon declared.

Dr Newberry remained silent but held Simon's stare, which seemed to infuriate him. In order to prevent another outburst I rose and surprised myself by saying, 'I'd like to see him.'

With a grunt Simon followed as Newberry led us along a short corridor and into an open plan intensive care unit. It was dimly lit and hushed save for the bleeping of machines and the swish of uniform as the staff went about their business. The heat clawed at my throat and I tried not to look at the comatose figures on the beds either side of me. At the far end of the room the nurse rose as we reached the last bed and stepped away to allow us privacy.

I felt my body tense and hoped that Simon hadn't noticed it. I silently urged myself to breathe steadily and to keep calm. As my eyes fell on the motionless figure lying on the hospital bed I experienced a shock. Surely this wasn't the man who had bullied me for most of my childhood, who had made me feel so inadequate? There were no clear blue eyes boring into me accusingly, no sardonic smile, no disdainful or pitying looks. It was fifteen years since I had seen my father and it was that final image that had stayed with me. Here in front of me now was a frail body, the grey face lined, the thin, wispy white hair flattened against a narrow egg-shaped head, bristle on the chin, chest skeletal.

I turned away feeling angry, not that my father should end up like this but for all the years I'd wasted being afraid of him, of living in awe and terror of him, yet he was nothing but flesh and blood after all, just like the rest of us.

I heard Simon hurrying after me. 'You're leaving?'

'There's nothing I can do here.'

'I'll have to come back tomorrow to hear what this consultant has to say unless you…'

'I can't,' I said sharply, feeling the panic rising.

I didn't want to be with my father. I didn't want to be in London. There were too many memories here for me. This was where Alison was buried and this was where I had experienced my mental breakdown after her death.

'I don't see why not. I'm very busy, Adam.'

'So am I,' I retorted, and I was. Jack was relying on me to get to the truth. When I had needed a friend he had been there. I wasn't going to let him down.

Simon said, 'At least have a drink. After all we haven't seen each other for years.'

I stared at him for a moment wondering what had brought about this volte face. Simon, like father, had been unsympathetic over my breakdown. As far as they had been concerned I had shamed the family name. Curiosity got the better of me and I said, 'OK.'

We found a wine bar around the corner from the hospital in Belvedere Road. It was already fairly crowded with people getting into the Christmas spirit. There was little chance that Faye would come here; the office and flat were in Convent Garden. If Father died I would have to tell her about him and Simon. Just one more secret I had kept from her and one more lie. As far as Faye was concerned I had no family. And I had never breathed a word to her about Alison or my breakdown. From the beginning of our relationship I had known that Faye wouldn't understand. It wasn't until now though that I admitted it to myself. I felt the stirrings of unease where my feelings for Faye were concerned. Over recent months we had drifted apart. I told myself it was because of her working in London and the demands of her new job, but I knew it had nothing to do with that.

Simon returned from the bar with a bottle of wine and a coke. I took the coke. We found a table in a dark corner near the gents' toilet as more people came in shaking out umbrellas and pulling off raincoats.

'You realise he might not be able to return home,' I said. 'He'll probably have to go into a nursing home.' And how he would hate that, I thought. He'd always despised illness of any kind seeing it as weakness and often self-inflicted.

'That will cost a bloody fortune,' grumbled Simon. He poured himself a large glass of red wine and drank almost half of it in one go.

'You can sell the house. It should fetch quite a price.'

'You haven't seen it. It's falling to pieces.'

And I didn't want to see it, ever.

Simon sniffed. 'I suppose you'll leave all that to me to arrange?'

His eyes bored into mine. If he was trying to intimidate me then he was failing. I remained silent. I guessed this was the purpose behind Simon's invitation. He wanted to dump all this on me. After a moment Simon was forced to continue.

'Harriet will have to see to it. She's got plenty of time now the children are at boarding school.'

I had scored a minor victory. 'How is Harriet?' I had vague recollections of a tall, slim girl with an oval face, perfect complexion and long straight blonde hair. I had no recollections of her personality.

Simon helped himself to another large glass of wine. 'She's all right.'

The conversation ground to a halt. I didn't know what to say to him. We were like strangers. What was I doing here wasting time? Into my mind flashed those seven letters SIEDNGO. What other words could I get out of them apart from GOD and DIES? SIGN? SIGNED? Why had Jack signed it 4th July 1994? That must have some significance. What had happened on that date? Perhaps I should look it up in an almanac or on the Internet?

Someone laughed uproariously at a nearby table startling me out of my reverie. I saw Simon's disapproval. I guessed this wasn't his sort of place.

'Are you still involved in research?' I asked. I knew he was but if I could keep him talking about himself it wouldn't give him time to pry into my affairs.

'Don't you ever read the newspapers?'

'Not unless I have to.' I said evasively, taking a swig of my coke.

'We're working on a number of projects: treatments for osteoporosis, obesity and cancer. That's why I can't spare the time up here, Adam. It's a race against the clock to develop the vaccine or drug before anyone else does and before the money runs out.'

I thought of that charity cycle ride photograph and Rosie's words. Three of the fire fighters in the photograph had died of cancer.

'You really think you can come up with something to help cure cancer?' I asked.

'Cure? No. Treat, yes, or perhaps a vaccine

for certain types. And that's the trouble there are so many different forms of cancer and so many different causes. It's not just down to genetics; the environment is to blame for many cancers.'

'How?'

'Exposure to synthetic chemicals, natural toxins, industrial processes, drugs, and viruses not to mention sunlight. Twenty to thirty percent of all cancers are caused by occupational exposure.'

Could those fire fighters have been exposed to something during the course of their jobs? Is that why they had contracted cancer? Or was it a matter of bad luck.

'What are the statistics for contracting cancer?'

'One in three.'

That high! Out of eight men on that bicycle three had contracted cancer, slightly higher than Simon's statistics but not so unusual.

'There's money in research, Adam. You should have finished your degree. Nothing was ever proven over Alison's death.'

I felt myself tense. I had wondered how long it would take Simon to remind me of my failure. Perhaps that was why I hadn't wanted to come here. I knew it was one of the reasons I'd cut myself off from my family. Alison's death had been an accident I told myself. She had fallen from that window. Only trouble was I couldn't remember a thing about it. The first I could recall was sitting in a police interview room.

Simon said, 'You shouldn't have let it ruin your career.'

'I didn't,' I replied tersely.

'You call painting a career?' Simon said, with barely disguised contempt.

I stiffened. His tone reminded me of Father's taunts to Mother over a hobby that had given her so much pleasure, and for which she'd had a talent. As far as my father was concerned art was futile. Simon clearly was of the same opinion even though he'd married an art historian.

'How did you know?' I asked. I hadn't told him or Father.

Suddenly Simon looked ill at ease. 'Harriet saw something about you in one of her art magazines,' he said, airily. 'Do you make any money out of it?'

'We get by.'

'We?'

'I'm married.'

Simon arched his eyebrows but I was spared his cryptic remark by the arrival of our meal.

After the waiter had left us I asked a question that had been bugging me almost since he had called me. 'How did you find me?'

'Your number was in Father's book?' he said a shade too quickly.

'It couldn't have been. Father doesn't have it.'

'Then you must have given it to me at some time,' Simon dismissed impatiently.

'Hardly.'

'Does it matter?' Simon said in exasperation. I held his stare, and I could see apprehension. 'Look, I got my secretary to track you down. She must have found your number in the telephone book, or through directory enquiries. Harriet said the article mentioned you were living on the coast, in Portsmouth, so it wasn't that difficult to run you to earth. I thought you ought to know about Father even though you and he didn't hit it off.'

I let it go. We were ex-directory, so why had he lied and so obviously? Maybe he didn't care? Maybe he thought his younger brother dull and stupid? But then, I thought, I was being paranoid and overly suspicious. Jack's death and the subsequent events were making me see hidden motives where there was none.

I gazed across the restaurant and with a shock found myself staring straight into the eyes of the young motorbike rider whom I'd seen on the seafront yesterday. This time there was no mistaking it, he was looking right at me and it wasn't with affection. I held his intense and hostile glare as best I could. He didn't flinch or glance away. He was dressed in the same red and black leathers as yesterday, his lean face was unshaven. I had been right the first time: there *was* something familiar about him but it eluded me. Why was he so interested in me? Why didn't he approach me? He must have followed me here. This couldn't be a coincidence. Did he have something to do with Jack's death? Only one way to find out.

I scraped back my chair. Simon looked up at me in surprise. 'Gents,' I said, but the people at the table in front of us decided to leave at the same time blocking my path and when it was clear the young man had gone. I crossed to the toilet scanning the bar and the restaurant but there was no sign of him and neither was he inside the gents.

'I must be going,' I said abruptly on my return. Perhaps I could catch up with him outside.

Simon shrugged. He seemed to have lost interest in me, probably because he could see that I wasn't going to play his game. He said, 'I'll call you tomorrow to let you know how he is.'

It was my turn to shrug. I stepped outside and peered down the street. There was no motorbike and no young man. Damn!

I turned up Chicheley Street towards the river my mind full of questions. It had stopped raining. I came out by Waterloo Pier; behind me the lights glowed on the London Eye. The grinding of the London traffic mingled with the screeching of the trains as they shunted across the bridge from Waterloo to Charing Cross station. I turned left towards Westminster Bridge with the River Thames on my right. A boat hooted, someone laughed and I could hear a flute playing, a busker by the bridge I guessed.

The Thames made me think of the postcard Jack had sent me. I pulled it out of my pocket. The picture was one of the most famous in the world and one of my favourites. Turner had captured the warship, *Temeraire*, as it was being towed up the Thames to be broken up. She had fought so bravely at the Battle of Trafalgar and in Turner's picture she looks naked without her sails, suffering the humiliations of being shepherded up the river by a squat tug belching orange from its thin dark funnel. Had Jack meant anything by sending me this particular postcard or was it one he just happened to buy? Until I cracked that code I wouldn't know.

I turned my thoughts to the motorbike rider. Had *he* broken into Jack's house? Had Jody Piers' landlady seen him? Jody hadn't called me so I guessed not. I felt a stab of disappointment before I told myself not to be so stupid. I had met her once. I knew nothing about her. I was married.

Maybe I should report the motorbike rider to the police? Maybe I should tell Steve Langton about Jack's fears? Questions, questions and I should be in Portsmouth finding the answers not here staring over the murky waters of the Thames towards to the illuminated Houses of Parliament opposite.

I threw a couple of quid into the busker's cap, got a nod of thanks from the man and the lift of an eye from the dog and headed back home.

CHAPTER 4

When I arrived home I found that Rosie had left a message on my answer machine asking me to call round urgently. I glanced at the clock. It was too late to visit her now. I would have to wait until the morning. I wondered if she'd discovered more about Stella Hardway, the mysterious woman that Jack was supposed to be having an affair with. I tried to get her name from the letters on the postcard but even if I included all of them and not just the letters that Jack had underlined, I was still missing a 'W'.

As I rode down to Rosie's the next morning I checked my mirrors for any sign of the mysterious motorbike rider. There was none. I vowed that next time I wouldn't let him get away.

I kicked down the stand and glanced at Rosie's neighbour's house. There was no sign of life behind the windows. I hesitated over knocking, then thought what the heck! There was no answer. I climbed over the small dividing wall and rang Rosie's bell.

Her face was tired and drawn as she let me in. I followed her through to the lounge.

'I had a telephone call from the hospital yesterday afternoon,' she said, without preamble. 'Jack had cancer.'

I felt as though someone had thrown a bucket of icy water over me. Simon's words returned to me – the odds of contracting cancer were one in three. There were eight men on that bicycle photograph and four of them had contracted cancer. The odds had just increased. But how many were on the watch? Fourteen? Twelve?

Tears filled her dark eyes. 'Jack had an appointment to see the consultant. His secretary telephoned me to ask why he hadn't kept it.'

I wrestled with this news. Why hadn't Jack told me? Why hadn't he told his wife? It could explain Jack's last message to me, but not why he thought he was being followed, or the missing items.

'What kind of cancer?' If it was brain cancer then maybe that had caused Jack to have delusions.

'Non-Hodgkin's Lymphoma. I called our GP and she said that Jack came to her six months ago with a lump on his neck. She referred him to a consultant who did a biopsy, X Ray and CT scan. Jack paid privately. This must have been why he was so withdrawn and nervy. He didn't want me to know. He didn't want me to worry. Oh, the silly man. What he must have gone through. It makes me so angry that he felt he couldn't confide in me.'

The anguish in her eyes tore at my heart.

She said, 'I think Stella Hardway must be someone at the hospital.'

'Did you ask?'

'No.'

I could see that she didn't want to, but I could.

She began to cry. I went swiftly to her and took her in my arms. I felt a surge of anger with Jack for shutting her out of an important part of his life, as well as betrayed that Jack had chosen not to confide in me either.

'Why didn't he tell me?' She looked up at me with her tear-stained face.

I couldn't answer her, not yet. Maybe one day soon I might be able to.

Simon had said that occupational exposure counted for many cancers. Was that the connection? Had Jack and his colleagues been exposed to something that could have given them cancer? I felt a frisson of excitement run through me. I knew I was on the right track.

'Any good at ciphers?' I asked Boudicca, when I returned home an hour later. She looked up at me as if to say, 'You must be joking.'

I called the consultant's secretary; Rosie had given me her name, and asked her if she knew anyone called Stella Hardway. She didn't. I called the oncology department and the main switchboard of the hospital with the same result. Then I telephoned St Thomas's. Father was comfortable but still unconscious.

I played around with the letters that Jack had underlined ending up with twenty-one separate words. None of them meant anything to me. I stared at the paper strewn across the kitchen. Faye would have a fit. Which reminded me…

'You sound as if you're in a pub,' I said when she answered her mobile.

'Wine bar actually. We're with clients.'

'Stewart with you, is he?' I wasn't jealous. Maybe I should have been. In my mind's eye he was slick, sophisticated and good-looking, everything I wasn't.

'Yes.' Her voice sounded wary with a small note of petulance that warned me I'd be skating on thin ice if I pursed that angle.

'I won't keep you, just wanted to check you were OK.'

'I'm fine, what about you? All set for the exhibition? You haven't been drinking, have you?'

'You make me sound like an alcoholic,' I snapped.

'There's no need to be so touchy.'

I took a deep breath. 'No. I'm fine, everything's fine.'

I rang off before she could say anything further. I felt irritated. I told myself it was because of this damn puzzle rather than Faye's accusatory and derisory tone.

'Why did Jack put Rosie's name in inverted commas?' I asked Boudicca who was pushing her head up against my legs and meowing fit to bust.

Because it's her name, stupid!

A name. Of course! The code was a name and it wasn't bloody Stella Hardway.

I snatched up a piece of paper: Sid, Ned, Sine, Des, Denis, Denise, Enid…Did any of these have a connection with Jack, or with the fire fighters on Red Watch? Had I ever heard Jack mention any of them? No.

I wracked my brains. I walked about. I fed Boudicca. I made a coffee. Still nothing came to me. I was beginning to feel deflated. Back to square one.

I flicked on Radio Four. They were talking about the Man Booker Prize winner. Books. I froze. The books on Jack's study floor. The books I had replaced on the shelf. With a pounding heart I stared at the letters. God! It was so simple. GIDEONS. And on Jack's shelf had been a New Testament and Psalms. Half an hour later Rosie was opening the door to me again.

'Sorry to bother you, Rosie, but I think I dropped my pen when I was tidying Jack's study yesterday. I can't find it anywhere. Would you mind if I looked?'

'Of course.'

She didn't seem in the slightest bit suspicious. I guessed she was too tired and too upset.

I climbed the stairs with a racing heart hoping she wouldn't want to follow. She didn't. I reached for the small brown book that contained the New Testament and Psalms and read the inscription on the first page: 'Presented to Jack Bartholomew by The Gideons International within the British Isles, Date: December 1969.'

The date didn't tie up with the one on the postcard, but I knew it wouldn't. So, there had to be a reason why Jack had written 4 July 1994. Eagerly my fingers flicked through the thin pages until I found the Daily Readings. I turned to the 4th July, which referred me to the Acts Chapter 14 versus 1–18. Nothing. Holding my breath I flicked on to the next 4th July under the Daily Readings. This referred me to Psalms 10 versus 1-18.

'Is everything OK, Adam?' Rosie called up.

'Yes, fine.'

Psalm 10. I let out a long slow breath Jack had underlined a passage in verse 7 and in verse 8.

'Did you find it?'

'What?' I spun round, quickly slipping the small Bible into my pocket. 'No. I must have lost it elsewhere.' Had she seen me? I didn't think so. 'I might have dropped it in the studio or at the art gallery.'

I felt bad leaving her but I was itching to look at Jack's message. I felt less of a heel when she said that Sarah was due over shortly.

Instead of returning home I rode down to the seafront and ordered myself a coffee in the Blue Oasis Café. Through the window I could see the Hovercraft leaving a trail of white behind it as it skirted the tops of the waves on its way to the Isle of Wight. Lights were beginning to twinkle in Ryde across the water.

I eyed the occupants in the café. There was only an elderly couple in the corner. There was no sign of my pursuer, the motorbike man.

I took out my small pad usually reserved for sketching and a pencil from my jacket pocket and opened the New Testament and Psalms.

With my heart beating a little faster I transcribed the words Jack had underlined into my pad.

I looked up but no one was paying me any attention. I sat back to study what I had written.

His mouth is full of …deceit and fraud, he murder the innocent.

Whose mouth was full of deceit? Who had murdered the innocent? Had something happened in 1994 that had led to the cause of death of the innocent? Who were the innocent? I thought of that photograph pinned on my studio wall, of Jack who had been diagnosed with cancer and of the three men with him who had died of cancer. They were the innocent victims of something that had happened in 1994, something that had given them cancer. Jack had died trying to discover what it was. Jesus! Did I want to go on with this? Would I end up the same way as Jack? Is that why the motorbike man was following me? Waiting to see what I discovered, ready to make sure I had an accident when I got too close to the truth?

'I didn't have you down as a religious man.'

I started violently and then felt foolish as I saw Jody Piers, Rosie's neighbour, standing over me. My heart skipped a beat. 'Hello, what brings you here?'

'What do you think?' She pointed at her Lycra jogging pants and trainers, over the top of which she wore a waterproof jacket. Her hair was soaked and plastered to her small head. An earpiece from her personal CD player dangled on her narrow chest and she pressed a button to switch it off.

'You won't get very fit in here.'

'Oh bugger that, I'm glad of the excuse to stop. Not very dedicated, am I?' and she laughed.

I liked the sound of it, fresh and slightly wicked. She seemed genuinely pleased to see me and I felt flattered.

'I recognised your motorbike and here I find you with your nose buried in the good book.' She sat down heavily on the chair opposite. She stretched out her legs, which brushed against me. She seemed in no hurry to move and I was in no rush to protest. I was surprised to feel a languorous stirring in my loins before the guilt kicked in. I cleared my throat.

'Coffee?' I asked.

'Please. I'll forgo the doughnut though. I'll get a stitch running back.'

I pocketed the Gideons New Testament and Psalms and a few seconds later put the coffee in front of her.

'I'm glad I've run into you,' she said. 'I was going to call you.'

'Your landlady saw something?' I said, hopefully.

'She wasn't sure. There was a dark blue van parked outside but it could have been perfectly innocent.'

'She didn't get the make or registration number?'

She gave me a quizzical look. 'Why the interest? Is there something more to this break-in than you're telling me?'

She spoke lightly as though teasing me but my expression must have betrayed my concerns. She said, 'I can see there is.'

I hesitated, not sure whether to confide in her. It would sound fantastic. She'd think me paranoid, and why should I tell her anything? I didn't know her, though clearly she had known Jack and was on good terms with Rosie. But I had to tell someone and it wasn't going to be Faye. *Just as I had never told her about Alison.* It troubled me that I couldn't confide in my wife, but what was beginning to worry me more was the realisation that I never had been able to or even wanted to.

I put the postcard on the chrome table in front of her. 'What do you make of that?'

'It's a painting by Turner.' She picked it up and turned it over. I watched her expression turn from mild amusement to curiosity. 'It's from your friend and it reads like his last message.'

'It was. He posted that the day he died.'

She looked shocked. 'He *knew* he was going to die?'

'It seems incredible, but yes.'

She turned the postcard over in her slim hands frowning with concentration as she considered Jack's words. Finally she looked up and announced, 'It's a code.'

'And this is where it has led me.'

I pushed my sketchpad towards her. I could smell the scent of her body, which mingled with her sweat. It was a powerful aphrodisiac and again I felt the stirrings of desire. As if sensing my interest she peeled off her jacket and I could see her small breasts straining against the tight Lycra of her running top.

She said, 'What does it mean?'

I told her ending with, 'Jack must have been trying to find a connection between the cancer and something that happened in 1994 and my guess is that it was a fire or a chemical incident.'

I waited for her to tell me I was barking mad and provide some other simple explanation that hadn't yet crossed my mind. Instead a frown furrowed her brow, her green eyes were serious and her gaze intent.

In the silence I could hear the coffee machine whirring and gurgling. A radio was playing a Christmas tune and the door opened and shut letting in a blast of cold clammy air. The elderly couple left.

Finally she said, 'You think he was killed deliberately in that fire?'

I nodded. 'But don't ask me how.'

'This could be dangerous, Adam.'

I liked the way she said my name.

'Take it to the police and leave it to them,' she continued, firmly.

It was tempting and maybe she was right. I felt warmed by her concern. At the same time my stomach churned at the thought of entering a police station again. 'I'll talk to Steve Langton. He's a friend of Jack's and mine; he's a DI at the local police station.'

She seemed relieved at my decision. 'I'm sure that's the right thing to do.' She dashed a glance at her watch. 'I must be going. I've got a project to finish and a deadline looming. I'm doing a study of the marine life in Portsmouth harbour.'

Outside the door she hesitated. 'Will you let me know what the police say?'

I wanted to ask why. But maybe I already knew the answer.

'All right,' I agreed eagerly; it would give me a reason to see her again. I ignored the warning bells that were sounding in my head like Nôtre Dame's.

'You know where I live, number forty-two. Here's my telephone number.' She scribbled it in my sketchpad. 'But I might see you next week at your exhibition.'

I must have looked shocked or horrified.

She laughed and said, 'I'm based in the dockyard. I saw the posters outside the art gallery.'

'Well if you fancy venturing out on a cold winter's night and there's nothing on the television you're welcome to come to the private viewing on Saturday.'

'Great.' She plugged in her music. 'I'll see you then.'

Suddenly I was looking forward to the exhibition. I watched her lean body jog gracefully along the promenade towards the fun fair, then climbed on my bike and headed with trepidation for the police station.

Chapter 5

Fifteen years ago it had been a different police station in a different city but they, like hospitals, all have that same smell about them of disinfectant and fear. As soon as I stepped inside the lobby I could feel the sweat pricking my brow. As I waited to see Langton I ran my hands down the sides of my jeans, feeling the space around me growing ever smaller by the slowly ticking minutes. Soon I wouldn't be able to breathe. Maybe he wasn't in. Maybe I should simply turn and leave. But I forced myself to stay even as the memories flooded back and I was once again back in that bleak interview room in Oxford with the red-faced, heavily perspiring inspector and his baby-faced sergeant. *'What did you do, Adam?' 'Are you sure that's what happened?' 'You had a row with Alison, didn't you?' 'We have witnesses…' 'I didn't push her… I didn't… I didn't…'* Then nothing but darkness.

'Adam, come through.' Steve's confident, friendly voice catapulted me back into the present.

As the security door behind us closed, it sounded like the slamming of a prison cell.

I put one foot in front of the other and followed his purposeful athletic strides up the stairs to the first floor where I was shown into a modern office. I let out a breath, thankful that it had not the slightest similarity to an interview room.

'Drink?' Steve offered but I declined.

'I won't take up too much of your time,' I began but he waved away my concerns.

'I need a bit of a break and this lot's not going anywhere.' He indicated the pile of paperwork on his desk. I glanced at it as I sat down, seeing some rather grisly photographs of a woman who'd been attacked. They weren't very pleasant and I hastily looked away. The sounds of the station came to me from beyond Langton's closed door: footsteps hurrying, someone laughing, a telephone constantly ringing. Would he think me paranoid? I'd soon find out. I told him about the postcard and code, my last conversation with Jack, my theories on the break-in, the missing items, and what I thought Jack had been investigating. I watched for his reaction in the glow of the angle poise lamp on his desk. I needn't have bothered being a policeman he simply stared at me impassively.

'I know it sounds incredible, Steve, but something must have happened at a fire in 1994.'

'Lots of people die of cancer,' Langton said quietly.

'I keep telling myself that, but it doesn't feel right especially when you put it with everything else that has happened.'

'You want me to look into it.'

'Yes.'

After a moment, he said, 'I'm up to my eyeballs in work, Adam. You know what it's like at Christmas: more thefts, more fights, more domestics, more bloody everything and less coppers to handle it because of flu and colds.'

'So you're not going to do anything.'

'I'll talk to the officers who attended the break-in.'

I could see that was the best I was going to get, but I wasn't prepared to give up trying yet. 'Any further news on the fire that killed Jack?'

'No. It was just after four o'clock when it happened and dark. The old Labour club is tucked away behind the social security office. It's a bit off the beaten track for passers-by.'

'Perhaps someone working in the social security office saw something. Have you questioned them?'

'No, and we're not going to. I haven't got the manpower, Adam,' Langton added hastily. 'We put a flyer up on the staff notice board asking for anyone who saw anything to come forward but so far nothing and the media coverage didn't flush them out. It was probably kids.'

'And if it wasn't and Jack was the intended victim?' I said tersely.

'That just doesn't add up. How would the killer know that Jack would be the first into that building? Are you suggesting that one of his colleagues killed him?'

Steve was looking at me as if I should be carted

off to the nearest lunatic asylum. He was right, that was unthinkable. I said, 'Someone could have gained access to the fire station.'

'I know death is hard to come to terms with especially when it is someone close to us. We often look for someone to blame, but it was one of the hazards of his job.'

I could see that I wasn't going to convince him otherwise. I made one last attempt. 'And this code?'

'I'll check out the fire reports for 1994,' he said wearily.

I'd won an extra concession, but I was going to do that anyway, once Red Watch were back on duty, which was tomorrow.

I spent a restless night mulling over the message that Jack had left me before rising early the next morning. I recognised the fire fighter who answered the door to me from the wake. He was a tall, gangly man who resembled a giraffe with his long neck and rather prominent ears. He introduced himself as Pete Motcombe and took me upstairs to the kitchen where the fire fighters were seated around the large table taking a break before beginning the tasks and exercises of the day. As I looked at their solemn faces I understood what Steve Langton had meant. I felt ashamed for even thinking that one of them could have had something to do with Jack's death.

'Is it true that Jack's house was broken into on the day of the funeral?' Motcombe asked.

'Yes.'

A few expletives rumbled around the table.

'Was there much taken?' Motcombe asked.

'No, but I can't find Jack's diary or computer back-up disks. Would he have left them on the station?'

'They weren't in his locker. I haven't seen them.'

'It should have been me, not him.'

We all turned to stare at the owner of the anguished voice. He was in his late twenties with close-cropped hair and startling blue eyes that were filled with a sadness that tore at my heart.

'I was riding BA. I should have gone in first.'

Another man spoke, his voice gentle, 'Ian, you're not to blame. You mustn't torment yourself with that. It could have been any one of us.'

'I shouldn't have let him do it.'

'It was his job, Ian. He knew the risks just like

you do, like all of us know it.'

'But I swapped with him. Jack should have been pump man not me.'

'It was Jack who asked you to swap,' a female fire fighter I knew was called Sally said gently, pushing her fingers through her short blonde hair. 'You weren't to know what was going to happen.'

'When did you swap with Jack?' I asked Ian. Why hadn't Steve told me about this? Did he know? Was it important? Something in my gut told me it was.

'When he came on duty that morning. It was Jack ...'

He didn't get any further. The bells went down and suddenly I was left in the room alone with Motcombe who explained he was duty man.

'Ian's really cut up. Shouldn't be on duty,' Motcombe said. 'I've told him to see the doctor and get a sick note but he insists on being here. Why did you want to know about him swapping with Jack?'

I didn't want to give my real reason. I didn't see any need to worry these guys who were suffering the loss of their colleague. I said, 'I guess I'm finding it hard to come to terms with Jack's death, which is why I'm here really.' I plunged into the cover story that I'd worked out overnight. 'I want to paint something as a tribute to Jack.'

With surprise I realised that was exactly what I might do. 'Jack had three passions in his life: his family, his sailing and his job. Before I paint I like to research as much background as I can, immersing myself either in the period or the location or often both. I'm not sure what I shall paint yet, I just let ideas come to me by looking at everything associated with the subject, tucking things away in my sub conscious, getting a glimmer of an idea from an article, a photograph... I'm looking for some help on fire service background.'

'That sounds a great idea. Fire away.' Motcombe smiled at his pun.

'I thought I'd take the year 1994. It was when I first met Jack.' Strange but it hadn't struck me until then the significance of the date on the postcard. I couldn't immediately recall Jack talking about a dangerous incident in that year, or even on 4th July. Of course he might have used that date solely to draw me to the message in the New Testament and Psalms. I said, 'Can you tell me how many fire fighters would have been on the watch then and give me their names? I'd like to talk to them.'

'Sorry, can't help you. I wasn't on the watch and there's no one else left from that time. Or rather there's only Brian and he's convalescing in Devon.'

I was disappointed. I didn't really want to worry Brian with my enquiries.

Motcombe said, 'Des Brookfield might help you, though. He's at headquarters in Southampton.'

I knew that. 'Perhaps I could see the fire reports for that year. It would help me get a feel for the incidents that Jack attended.'

'They're kept at head office.'

I should have known. But at least I could kill two birds with one stone: speak to Brookfield and see the fire reports. I knew I must be following a trail that Jack had already trod. Had he found the report and made notes about it on his computer? Notes that someone had been very keen to erase all trace of. Only one more question to ask, and a delicate one, before heading for Southampton.

'Did Jack ever talk about a woman called Stella Hardway?'

Motcombe looked surprised. 'Name doesn't ring a bell. Why do you ask?'

'Rosie heard him talking to her and she wondered if anyone knew her address. She wanted to contact her to tell her about Jack, in case she hadn't heard.'

It was waffle but it seemed to satisfy Motcombe. 'I can't recall the name. I'll ask the others for you, if you like?'

'Thanks, but don't say anything to Rosie. She's got enough to cope with.'

I gave him one of my cards.

Thirty minutes later I was at fire service headquarters, ringing a bell at the deserted reception desk of the 1950s building that had the air of an old fashioned library about it. A few seconds later a woman in her mid fifties with short grey hair and a round figure appeared. I asked to see Brookfield.

'Adam.' Brookfield was striding across the parquet floor, a smile on his swarthy face that didn't touch his eyes and his arm stiffly outstretched. I took his hand returning the pressure, trying not to wince at the grip that was like iron.

'What brings you here?'

He waved me into a seat and I gave him the same story I'd spun Motcombe. He too was enthusiastic about the painting. When I mentioned that I had decided to focus on 1994 he said: 'I was on the watch then. Perhaps I can help you.'

If only he could. With a quickening heartbeat, I said, 'How many men were there on the watch?'

Brookfield's dark eyes narrowed as he thought back down the years. 'Fourteen usually, but if I remember correctly we were a couple of men down that year. We made up the numbers with different men on secondments from other stations. I was sub-officer and Stuart Hallington was leading fireman. He emigrated to New Zealand. As well as Jack there was Colin Woodhall, who's now running his own fire safety business in Turkey and doing very well for himself; Dave Caton lives in France; Sam Frensham has a hotel in the Cotswolds; Brian Clackton, who's still on the watch, and Sandy Ditton who works in Portsmouth. There was also Vic Rushmere, Scott Burnham, Duggie Leith and Tony Penfold, they've all since died of cancer.'

'Vic Rushmere had cancer?' He hadn't been

in the bicycle photograph and Rosie hadn't mentioned him.

'Yes. Did you know him?' Brookfield looked surprised. I had to be more careful about my reactions.

'No.'

'He was the first one to die, if I remember correctly. Bloody awful disease, cancer. Red Watch has had its fair share of bad luck.'

That was putting it mildly. If I needed convincing I was on the right track this was it. Five men out of twelve was definitely one man too many according to Simon's statistics. Even if I counted in the two secondments, it would still be a little over the odds.

'Do you have the addresses of any of them?'

Brookfield shook his head. 'No, and I doubt if personnel will give them to you, data protection and all that. Some of the others on Red Watch might know or you could put a notice up in the station.'

That was an idea, using my painting story as a reason for wanting to talk to them. 'What about Sandy Ditton? You mentioned he worked in Portsmouth.'

'At the Maritime Museum in the dockyard.'

I could at least speak to him. 'Would it be possible to see the fire reports for 1994?'

'I expect so but I'd have to get permission from the chief first.'

'How long do you think that will take?' I tried not to show my disappointment. I had hoped to look at the records then but I supposed that had been unrealistic.

'A couple of days. I'll see what I can do.'

'Do you remember any particularly big fires during that year, or any unusual or nasty ones?'

'Can't say that I recall anything out of the ordinary, just more of the same that we usually get: car and bin fires, false alarms, people stuck in lifts, chip pan fires. No, nothing that big, but in 1992 we had a major factory fire.'

'Do you keep a diary?' I tried not to sound as if I was clutching at straws but every word Brookfield uttered sent me into further gloom. I guessed I had been too optimistic to begin with. This wasn't going to be easy.

'No, and I don't keep a scrapbook either, though I know some of the fire fighters do.'

I'd forgotten about that. Did Jack have a scrapbook? If he did then had that gone missing too?

Brookfield said, 'I've never been one for looking back. Always ahead that's the only way. Sandy always kept a diary and he's got a mind like an elephant. Never forgets dates or events.'

At last someone who might remember, or who at least had kept a record. I brightened up at that.

Brookfield looked pointedly at his watch. 'I've got a meeting. Leave it with me, Adam, and I'll see what I can do about those fire reports. How can I get hold of you?'

Once again a card came out and I handed it to Brookfield.

I telephoned the Maritime Museum and asked to speak to Sandy Ditton only to be told he wasn't working until Monday afternoon. Directory enquiries said he was ex directory so I had no choice but to wait until then. That left me with Sam Frensham in the Cotswolds as the next nearest former Red Watch fire fighter to talk to.

I called Rosie.

Her first words were, 'Did you find out anything at the station?'

'Jack wasn't having an affair. He must have been talking to someone at the hospital.'

'Yes, that must have been it.' I heard the relief in her voice.

I asked her if Jack had kept a scrapbook. She said he hadn't. 'I want to get in touch with some of Jack's old colleagues. Do you know whereabouts in the Cotswolds Sam's hotel is?'

'Just outside Stow on the Wold. I can't remember what it's called though. It's ages since Jack and I went there. Sorry.'

'Don't worry. I can look it up. What about Sandy Ditton's address?'

'No. The only one I've kept in touch with from those days is Carol Rushmere and that's because she works as a part time admin officer at the school where I teach.'

At last, a stroke of luck. 'Can you tell me where she lives?'

'Why this interest, Adam?'

'It's just an idea I have, about doing a painting for Jack. I'd like to talk to Jack's old colleagues.'

'Oh, Adam.' Her voice broke and I felt a heel. Now I was committed to it, but I didn't mind. It was a good idea.

Rosie gave me Carol Rushmere's address. I glanced at my watch. It was just after one o'clock. Rosie had said Carol worked part time. There was a chance she'd be in and I was going to take it.

CHAPTER 6

Carol Rushmere was a tall, big-boned woman in her late fifties with extra weight around her midriff and hips. She had plump arms, a round face and neatly coiffured bottle blonde hair that seemed stuck in a 1960s time warp. Her wide blue eyes smiled cautiously at me as she offered me tea.

I accepted out of politeness and followed her through the narrow hallway into a small, modern kitchen that faced on to a crazy paved back yard hardly big enough to house the garden shed and washing line. It overlooked another row of small houses built in the 1970s.

'So you're a friend of Jack Bartholomew's. I was sorry to learn of his death. Poor Rosie.' She switched on the kettle and retrieved two mugs from a wooden mug stand. 'I'm not sure how I can help you with any painting, Mr Greene.'

'Jack was a very good friend to me, and I feel I need to paint something as a tribute to him.'

'I see,' she said, obviously not seeing, but prepared to humour me. 'Biscuit?'

'No thanks.' I took the mug of tea and followed her swaying hips through to the open plan lounge that ran the length of the house, and faced a busy road junction. They were building new houses in the grounds of the old psychiatric hospital opposite and the headlights from the heavy lorries transporting earth swept the room as they swung right, heading out of the town on to the dual carriageway. To the left of the large, picture window stood a decorated artificial Christmas tree with blinking coloured lights and a handful of wrapped presents underneath.

'I didn't know Jack that well,' she said. 'He was fairly new on the watch when Vic died.'

She took the chair to the right of me across the

fireplace where a small electric fire glowed behind a painted black surface with artificial coals. Christmas cards hung suspended above the mantelpiece on a piece of string that stretched from the corner of the room by the window to a tall glass fronted wall cabinet.

'When did your husband die, Mrs Rushmere?' I asked as gently as I could.

'May 24, 1996. He was only forty-six.'

The same age as Jack. There was silence for several moments, long enough for the brass carriage clock on the mantelpiece to become audible. I followed her gaze to the silver framed photograph beside the clock where I saw a man with a sharp jutting face, all angles and bones, but with a wide smile that softened it and eyes that sparkled.

'He had cancer, I believe.' I sipped my tea.

'Yes, skin cancer. It spread very rapidly, went to his liver and then his lungs.'

I could see by her expression that her mind had travelled back to the gruelling days when she had nursed him. Her hands were constantly on the move, touching her hair, stroking the side of her face or rubbing gently at her nose. I wasn't quite sure how to ask further questions about her husband's illness but as it was I didn't have to.

'It started with a blister, here.' She indicated the rear of her right ear lobe. 'It grew and turned into a large mole and that's when Vic first went to the doctor. After that the cancer seemed to spread very rapidly. He had chemotherapy and radiotherapy but it made no difference. I think it had already reached his liver by the time he was diagnosed.'

'When was that?'

'October 1995.'

Again that silence. I tried to think of how to phrase my next question without alerting her as to the real purpose of my visit. After a moment I said, 'Did he ever talk about any fires that he went to that were particularly dangerous, or he was concerned about afterwards?'

'A few: houses with Calor gas fires in them that exploded, much like it did with Jack, garage fires where there were oxyacetylene tanks, companies where chemicals were kept.'

'When was that?' My hopes rose only to be dashed by her next words.

'They happened all the time. I used to wave him off to work often wondering if it would be the last time I'd see him. I never expected him to die of cancer.'

'Did he keep a diary?'

'No. But he kept a scrapbook.'

Great! 'Have you still got it. I'd like to see it if I may. It would give me some background information and ideas.'

'Of course, if I can find where I put it.'

'You wouldn't have thrown it away?' I said alarmed.

'It's around somewhere. I'll look it out for you over the weekend and give you a call if you like.'

I liked, but would have wished for her to do it sooner. I once again gave out my card. At this rate I'd have to have a new print run.

On the doorstep I paused. 'Did your husband ever say anything to you about what he thought caused the cancer?'

'Too much sun when he were a kiddie lying on the beach all day probably.' She shrugged. 'Who knows what sets these things off?'

Who indeed I thought, climbing on my bike. My conversation with Carol Rushmere had opened up another source of information, however, and one I was cross with myself for not thinking of sooner.

The librarian told me that I had to book to use the microfiche but after a little gentle persuasion, when I could see that one had just become vacant, she led me to it and soon I was trawling back through the local newspaper for fire reports or accidents in 1994. I started with 4th July. My excitement was short-lived. There was no fire reported on that day. That didn't mean to say there hadn't been one, but if there had then it couldn't have been very significant.

I began to trawl through the rest of that month and soon realised that it was a mammoth task, since the local newspaper reported everything from a chip pan fire to a spate of arson attacks on parked cars. And the reports didn't usually mention which watch had attended the incident.

I jotted down a couple of major fires, one in April 1994 in a hotel just off the seafront, that had been before I had met Jack, and the other in a garage behind Elm Grove in November. I knew Red Watch had attended them because Brookfield was quoted as sub-officer. It was pointless though; I was simply going through the motions. It couldn't be those.

I wracked my brains trying to recall any fires in 1994, and particularly in July, which could have been responsible for causing cancer. Jack and I had spent every spare day out sailing. I remembered it as being a very hot month, and the newspaper reports I'd just read had confirmed it: continuous sun, soaring temperatures and air pollution warnings.

I gave it up. It was like searching for a pearl on the pebbled beach. I would have to wait for the incident reports, or perhaps Vic Rushmere's scrapbook might give me a lead.

I returned home feeling deflated. My mobile rang as I stepped inside the house. It was Simon, at last.

'You'd better come. They don't think he's got long.'

My heart gave a jolt. This was the end.

I scribbled a note to Faye saying I had to go out and wasn't sure when I would be back, fed Boudicca and once again left for London.

'You're too late. He died half an hour ago.' Simon greeted me in the same sterile waiting room as before. With those sharp words and disdainful look I saw what I had missed the first time: how like Father he had become.

Slowly his words sunk in. *He was dead.* The

slate was wiped clean. I didn't have to pretend or apologise anymore.

'Do you want to see him?' Simon continued.

Did I? There had been so many times in my life when I had fervently wished my father dead, but now that he actually was it didn't seem real. I couldn't quite believe it. I didn't know what to feel and I wouldn't until I saw him.

Simon said he'd wait for me outside the hospital. I pulled aside the curtains of the intensive care bed and stared at the pallid form. All the personality had been stripped from that gaunt, grey face. I told myself that the feelings of shame at having failed him, and the sense of inadequacy that had accompanied me all my thirty-six years, were finally over, even though I knew that you couldn't shake off years of conditioning in a matter of seconds. It would take more than my father's death to erase from my memory the look in his eyes when he'd come to the police station after Alison's death. I'd seen the doubt and the disgust. And I'd seen the contempt when he'd visited me in the clinic.

I tried to tell myself that there had been happier memories such as when he'd taken me to watch England play cricket against the Australians at the Oval. I couldn't think of many more. He had fed and clothed me though and paid for my education. I couldn't love him but I could feel sorry for how things had worked out. I hadn't wanted it this way. I caught up with Simon outside the hospital.

'Made your peace?' Simon said sarcastically, drawing on a cigarette.

I didn't answer him. My mind was trying to grapple with the surprising sensation that, despite myself, I was feeling sorrow. We began walking towards the car park.

'We'll need to sort out funeral arrangements,' Simon went on, as I remained silent. 'Harriet can do that. She can contact Father's old colleagues and put an announcement in *The Times* and *The Daily Telegraph,* though no doubt the newspapers will run an obituary.'

Yes, our father had been a successful and famous a chemist. I had tried to follow in his footsteps, but my degree in Physical Science had come to a premature and abrupt end with Alison's death.

I brought my attention back to Simon who was speaking. 'We'll need to find the will. Father kept a copy in his study. We could check that out now.'

'You keep saying "we" Simon.'

'He was your father too. You can hardly blame him for what happened to you.'

Can't I? The continuous pressure to achieve, the measurement of my every achievement against my brother's and the constant carping that I hadn't reached the required standard. But none of that mattered now. What a waste of the years.

Simon zapped open the door of his Range Rover and paused before climbing in. 'It would have to happen now, right when I'm in the middle of negotiations with an American syndicate for a big finance package. I can't afford to hang around up here, Adam. Timing is critical. It would help if you at least did something.'

I scrutinised him. He appeared to be telling the truth. With some reluctance, pulling on my gloves and helmet I said abruptly, 'OK. I'll meet you at the house.'

I arrived outside Father's house in Belgravia before Simon and managed to squeeze the bike in a small space not far from it. I knew he'd have trouble parking. I gave the engine a quick rev before switching it off, then kicked down the stand.

As the London traffic screeched around me I looked up at the four-storey house. It seemed dirtier and shabbier than I remembered. The whitened stone façade that faced the street on ground level had grown grubby with the London pollution and badly needed painting. The casement windows needed replacing, and paint was flaking off the black iron railings that formed a small forecourt and which also surrounded the balcony giving off from the first floor long sash windows.

I locked my helmet in the box on the bike. I had agreed nothing with Simon, though Simon probably thought I had by coming back here. I didn't want to go inside the house but I knew I had to. Other memories would assail me: my mother's strained face and lean body, her haunted sad eyes. The smell of her soft perfume and her gentle smile were always overshadowed by those last few years of her life and my father's lack of understanding and intolerance towards illness. I felt panic fingering my throat but before it could get a hold Simon was striding towards me.

The house smelt of age and neglect. Simon climbed the stairs muttering something about a drink. I headed for the kitchen. It hadn't changed:

the cracked enamel sink, the ancient built-in oak cabinets with frosted glass, the pine table in the centre of the room with four chairs around it. There was crockery on the drainer under a red and white striped tea towel.

I crossed to the french windows and gazed out on to a narrow strip of garden but it was too dark to see anything save the tall, wavering trees in the ill-tempered wind.

'Whisky?' Simon returned, waving a half full bottle.

'No thanks.'

'Well here's to the old man.' Simon tossed the drink back in one go and poured himself another. Picking up the almost full bottle he said, 'Might as well get this over with.'

Father's study smelt of stale tobacco and dust. The heavy oak furniture, shelves of dusty books, brown edged papers and dark velvet curtains all served to make me feel claustrophobic. I could hear my father's brittle voice. *'I'm disappointed in you, Adam. To think a son of mine should suffer a mental breakdown. We've certainly never had anything like this in **my** family'.*

Lawrence Greene would make no allowance for the loss of my mother when I was nine, the pressure he had piled on me, and Alison's death. Counselling and psychotherapy were for wimps. In that battered grey metal filing cabinet in the far right-hand corner by the window were my father's private papers including the reports on my progress from the psychiatrist. I needed to retrieve them but didn't want to do so in front of Simon.

Simon was sitting at father's desk going through his drawers. 'Ah here it is. I thought he might have given it to the solicitor.' Simon extracted a document from a slim manila envelope.

I didn't need to be a mind reader to know what Father's will contained; I could see it in Simon's expression.

'It's all right,' I said, pre-empting him. 'You don't have to tell me. He's left me nothing.'

'I'm sorry, Adam.'

'I bet, you are,' I threw at him. 'Do I even need to ask who inherits?'

Simon shrugged.

'Fine. Good bye, Simon.'

'Where are you going?'

'Home, of course.'

'Aren't you going to stay and –'

'Help you? You've got to be joking.'

'There's no need to be so bitter.'

'I'm not.' And I meant it. I didn't want Father's money, but neither did I see any need to hang around and help Simon. Besides I had other more important things to do. I had to find out about this fire in 1994. I was pinning my hopes on Vic Rushmere's scrapbooks and those fire reports, yet I wondered if there was more I could do.

'Let me know when the funeral is,' I tossed over my shoulder as I left.

Before I knew it I was riding through the traffic lights at Hindhead. It was then I noticed the motorbike behind me. It kept a steady distance, but I could tell it was following me. I slowed and it slowed. I squinted in my mirrors to get a better look at it but it was dark and raining. Was it the same motorbike I'd seen along the promenade? Was it the young man I'd seen in the restaurant when I was with Simon?

I felt my pulse begin to race. What to do now? I could hardly turn round and ride back towards him. Perhaps if I pulled in he would overtake me. Perhaps he would stop. There was nowhere to pull over here but I knew that not far ahead the road became a dual carriageway and just as it did there was a derelict building on the left that had once been a roadside café. I could pull in there and see what he did. If it was the unshaven young man then it was about time he told me why he was stalking me.

There it was, just ahead, not far now. I sped up, my eyes on that derelict building looking for somewhere to pull in. Suddenly a car shot out of nowhere. Jesus! I swung the bike to the right to avoid colliding with it, across the other side of the road, fighting to keep it upright, my heart slamming against my ribs fit to burst. A van was coming towards me, lights blazing horn blaring. I swerved back to my left on to the correct side of the road with inches to spare as the van roared past. With my breath coming in gasps, and my head pounding, I eased the machine over in front of the derelict café and switched off the engine. I wrenched off my helmet and let the rain lash against my face. I took in gulps of air and waited for my heart rate to settle down. Eventually I became conscious of the cars racing past me. I spun round, there was no one else parked and the motorbike had vanished.

When I arrived home Faye was in the lounge.

I went straight to the kitchen and poured myself a large glass of whisky half of which I downed in one go. Faye joined me and looked pointedly at the glass. I thought if she so much as utters one word about my drinking so help me I'll throw the bloody glass at her. She opened her mouth to speak but must have seen the warning in my expression because she closed it again and moved across to the cooker.

'I can put a pizza in the oven if you're hungry. I ate lunchtime at a client meeting.'

Food was the last thing on my mind. I could have been killed. I very nearly was. Where the hell had that Mercedes come from? It must have shot out of a side road. Had it been waiting there for me? But no, that was ridiculous.

'Did you hear me, Adam?'

'I'm not hungry,' I muttered, tossing back the rest of the whisky, feeling the warmth slide down my throat and wrap itself around my heart. It stilled my nerves but not my racing mind. Now I was beginning to settle down I wanted to think through the incident rationally and calmly. First though I had a job to do. I guessed it wasn't going to be easy but I couldn't put it off any longer. I had to tell Faye about my father. If I didn't then

Faye might find out from Simon. How could I guarantee that she wouldn't be here when he or Harriet called about the arrangements for the funeral?

I poured myself another whisky. Faye tutted. I said, ' Before you say anything about this,' I waved the glass at her, 'there's something you should know.' The words froze in my throat. It wasn't that I was so upset that I couldn't speak; I just didn't know how to *begin* to tell her something that I should have spoken about ten years ago, when we first met.

My silence only served to increase her agitation. 'Something's gone wrong with the exhibition?' I heard the alarm in her voice.

'It's not the exhibition. I've just returned from London…'

'But you never go to London, you hate it there.' She was looking at me now with a mixture of trepidation and anger.

'I had no choice. My father's dead.'

'You haven't got a father.'

'I have. And a brother, called Simon. My father passed away this afternoon.'

For once I had rendered her speechless. I tossed back the whisky. 'I didn't tell you because I've been estranged from my family for fifteen years.'

I held my breath waiting for her to ask why. There was no way I was going to tell her about Alison or my breakdown. Eventually, she would find out. Husbands shouldn't have secrets from their wives, least not like mine. It wasn't right not if you really loved one another…

She said, 'Why didn't you tell me this before? Why lie to me?'

'I didn't mean to lie. I just didn't want to speak about it. I had cut myself off from them.'

'What else haven't you told me?'

Quite a lot, I thought, but didn't say. She hadn't offered her condolences but I didn't hold that against her. My surprising news had probably driven it from her mind, or at least that's what I told myself.

'My father has left everything to Simon.' I could see she was grappling with this new information. 'I shall attend the funeral and that will be it.'

'How much has he left?'

'Does it matter?'

'Well of course it does. You're his son.'

'I don't know.'

'Where in London did he live?'

'Belgravia.'

'Those houses are worth a fortune!'

'It's not in a very good state of repair.'

'You can't let your brother take everything, that's not fair. You should have told me about your family before. You've as much right to your father's money as he has. Just think what we could do with it.'

I could feel my anger rising. 'I don't want to talk about it.'

'You're going to have to, Adam. With that kind of money we could buy a decent apartment in London.'

'I don't want an apartment in London.'

'You said that after this exhibition you'd consider it. Here's a golden opportunity and you're going to let it go past,' she said crossly.

'I am not living in London.' I shouted.

'And that's it! What about me? Don't I get a say in this? I'm the one who has to work there and travel back and forth. You can paint anywhere.'

'That's just it, Faye, I can't. I can't even paint here.' My anger subsided as quickly as it had risen. It was only then that I knew how much I hated this house, and how I loathed being even five miles away from the sea. Before I had met Faye I had lived opposite it, in a studio apartment at Old Portsmouth.

'So what are all those images of the Festival of the Sea that we're exhibiting? Rubbish?'

'They're mediocre.' I moved away from her. I needed space. I tried one more time to make her understand. 'I need to be near the sea, Faye. I need to breathe it, smell it, taste it. I need to see and feel it in all its moods, all its seasons.' She was staring at me as if I'd gone mad. 'This house is wrong.'

'Then move.'

'Not to London.'

'We can have a place in London and an apartment here but we can't do that without your father's inheritance. Have you any idea of house prices these days? You haven't exactly been earning a lot in the last couple of years.'

'Jesus, Faye! You really know how to hit a man when he's down, don't you?'

'Well it has to be said, Adam. My job's kept us living here and allowed you to paint…'

She nearly said it but snapped her mouth shut before she could. I heard her unspoken words *'instead of getting a proper job'*. I turned away.

'What's happened to you, Adam? You've become so selfish?'

I didn't answer. There wasn't much I could say to that. I went to the studio. I picked up Jack's postcard. Turner had been a genius: creative, imaginative, and innovative. Everything I aspired to. Was Turner's 'The Fighting *Temeraire*' trying to tell me something? She was a warship. This was her last journey, is that why Jack had chosen it? Had he had known that this would be his final quest?

I studied the painting: the brilliant sunset reflected in the water at the end of the day. I thought of Jack, of Alison and my father, their days had ended. I thought of my near miss on the way home from London. I knew it had been no accident. Whoever had been driving that Mercedes had intended killing me. It had almost been the end of my days too. He hadn't succeeded but I had no doubts that whoever it was would try again.

CHAPTER 7

Saturday night and I stared at my paintings in the ancient stone warehouse that had been converted to an art gallery and despised every single one of them, wondering if I was the only person who saw their faults. How could I not when the image of 'The Fighting *Temeraire*' burned in my brain?

The room was crowded and hot. I nodded at people and even spoke to some but I was on automatic pilot. When I wasn't thinking about Jack, and that Mercedes, I was thinking about my father's funeral. I was cursing myself for walking out on Simon when I had. I should have extricated my files from that cabinet. I could have got Simon out of the study long enough to do so. Now I would have to wait until the funeral. By which time he might have gone through the file. I didn't relish the fact of him knowing all about my sessions with the psychiatrist. His superior attitude would be more than I could stomach.

I gazed around the room with a glass of wine in my hand. Everyone seemed to be having a good time and quite a few people had congratulated me. I was disappointed that Jody hadn't shown up but there was time yet.

My eyes alighted on Faye. She was elegantly dressed in a short midnight blue dress; her straight blonde hair was glowing after the three hours she'd spent in the hairdressers that morning and her silver jewellery showed off her fair flawless skin to perfection. She caught my eye, raised her glass and smiled at me. No one would have guessed that we had spent the day in a sullen silence, only communicating when we had to.

Her gesture reminded me of my first exhibition

in 1996. I had met Faye through the marketing agency the art gallery had engaged to help promote themselves and promising artists. My paintings had formed only part of the exhibition, but it was mine that Faye had chosen to promote through magazine reviews and articles. She said that my dark, lean looks would photograph well. The brooding young artist was how she had positioned me. I was dark, yes, and lean but I was silent because I was shy, totally uncomfortable with crowds. I couldn't tell her then that I had suffered a complete breakdown because I sensed she would run a mile and I needed her. Not for her ability to promote me but because I had fed off her self-confidence. I had gorged myself on her strength. She boosted my ego and it had needed a lot of boosting. I had felt that with Jack's friendship and Faye's love I could finally close the door on my past. Stupid.

I smiled back at Faye; it was an effort. I wasn't as good an actor as she was. She was talking to the tubby little Lord Mayor, exuding self-confidence and bonhomie. She'd already telephoned one of her lawyer friends in London to ask how we stood about contesting the will. If there was a way then I had every confidence that

Faye would find it, but I didn't want a penny of father's money. I also didn't want her attending the funeral, but I couldn't see how I could keep her away from it.

'Wonderful exhibition, Adam.' A voice broke through my thoughts and I found Nigel Steep, the manager of the commercial port, beside me. He was a rotund man, immaculately turned out in navy blazer and khaki-coloured slacks with a crease in them that made your eyes water.

'I'm glad you like them.'

'We're going to buy a couple to hang in our reception.'

I laughed. 'I would have thought you'd got enough by me already.' I'd previously been commissioned to paint the scenes from the bustling port.

'Never can have too much of a good thing,' he chuckled. 'It's an investment.'

'Then you'd better get in quick before Faye's friend from London snaps them up,' I said, tossing my head in the direction of Faye and a tall, snakelike man dressed from head to toe in black relieved only by a yellow spotted bow tie. I pointed Nigel in the direction of Martin, the gallery manager, who was conversing with the waiters and he bustled off to speak to him.

I began to circulate, nodding at this person, making the occasional remark to another but it was agony for me. Faye was giving me the evil eye, though, so I had better do my best.

The door opened. I hoped it would be Jody but it was a slight man with limp brown hair. He was flanked by two burly men in smart suits. His eyes scanned the room but Faye, who has an inbuilt antenna when it comes to spotting VIPs, was beside him in a flash with her outstretched hand. The Lord Mayor had been hastily dumped on a woman with a hairstyle that reminded me of Margaret Thatcher, and which appeared to be rigidly held in place with enough hair spray to cause a hole in the ozone layer. Faye glanced over her shoulder and beckoned to me and reluctantly, like a recalcitrant schoolboy, I sidled across the room.

'Darling, this is the Right Honourable William Bransbury, Minister for the Environment, Energy and Waste,' Faye introduced brightly. I knew who he was.

'Thank you for coming,' I said dutifully, surprised to find his handshake rather weak.

'Not at all. I'm very pleased to be invited. It's

good to support local talent and I hear you have quite a reputation as a marine artist.'

His voice was rather high and nasal, and he looked nervous as his hazel eyes flickered around the room. Maybe he didn't like these events, a considerable handicap for a politician, I thought. I had expected someone more self-assured. Perhaps television made them appear like that.

'Would you like a drink, Minister?' Faye beckoned one of the waitresses.

Bransbury took the glass of white wine. 'How about showing me round?'

'Of course.' I was somewhat surprised, but Faye seemed pleased.

I found myself with a small but growing entourage, as I explained the paintings that had commemorated the 200th anniversary of the Battle of Trafalgar: the private yachts lining the pontoon at Gunwharf Quays with hundreds of coloured flags flying from the halyards; the elegance and majesty of the tall ships, the working boats and warships from the Royal Navy and from around the world, and the little private leisure craft bobbing on the azure blue of the Solent amidst the Isle of Wight ferry and the hovercraft. Suddenly into my mind once more came the image of Turner's painting of the *Temeraire*. She had been active at the Battle of Trafalgar. Was that why Jack had chosen to send me that particular postcard? Was there some connection with my exhibition? Had the fire been in an art gallery or at an exhibition? Then it clicked. Nelson's flagship, HMS *Victory,* was here, in the Historic Dockyard. The fire that Jack was referring to must have been in the dockyard. I almost cried out with excitement. I was right, damn it. I had to be. I wanted to rush away and check. I could barely contain my impatience.

Bransbury said, 'What are you working on at present?'

With an effort I dragged my mind back to the politician. 'I'm thinking of painting something as a tribute to a close friend of mine, Jack Bartholomew. He was a fire fighter. He was killed in an arson attack.'

'I read about it in the newspapers. Poor man, quite tragic.'

Who could tell me about a fire in the dockyard? My eyes shifted away from Bransbury towards the door, standing just inside it was Jody. My heart lurched and all thoughts of escaping vanished from my mind. I glanced around guiltily in case Faye had witnessed my transformation but she was busy talking to her London friend with the bow tie. Jody spotted me, and the way her face lit up sent a rush of blood through my body and filled me with a desire that I hadn't experienced since Alison. Jody was making a beeline for me. Now all I had to do was ditch the politician.

'Hi.'

'Hello,' I smiled back at her. She was dressed in brown casual trousers and a tight fitting green cashmere cardigan setting off the colour of her eyes, which were smiling into mine with a hint of mischief that made my heart race. Around her smooth, slender neck was a bronze medallion necklace and she wore small amber droplet earrings. Her chestnut hair was spiky, she wore a hint of lipstick, and a trace of mascara accentuated her almond-shaped eyes. I cleared my throat, and remembering my manners introduced her to the politician.

'I know the Minister,' Jody replied rather tersely. 'And his stance over the proposed development of Langstone Harbour.'

Bransbury looked uncomfortable, but Faye came to his rescue.

'You've hogged the Minister long enough, darling,' she said laughing whilst glaring at me. Then her eyes swivelled to Jody. I saw a slight narrowing of her pupils and a minute rise of her finely plucked eyebrows. If Jody noticed it she didn't let on; she was looking at Faye with undisguised interest.

I introduced my wife to Jody, and, after a rather frosty 'hello,' Faye turned her back on her, and swept Bransbury away.

'I'm sorry if Faye was a little hostile,' I began but Jody smiled.

'Was she? I didn't come here to see her.'

'What *is* the Minister's stance on the harbour?'

'He's for development. I'm against it like a good many people, but money talks unfortunately. Still nothing's settled yet and the environmental lobby are very strong. Anyway, I haven't come here to talk about that or him. Are you going to give me the guided tour?'

'Love to, but I warn you I've just bored the pants off the Minister.'

'From what I can see they look fantastic. The paintings, that is, and not the Minister's pants.'

This time I found the tour a pleasure rather than a chore. I liked the sensation of being close to her. I liked the way she moved: slowly, casually, languorously like a contented cat. I felt some of my old enthusiasm about my paintings returning, which made me more talkative than usual and hotter. Or was that just the wine and the fact of being so close to her? The rest of the people in the room seemed to fade away.

'Did you go to the police about Jack's death?' she asked when we had finished and were standing alone. More people had come in and the room was squeezed tight with bodies. I was surprised to realise it didn't bother me in the least.

'Yes, for all the good it did me.'

'They didn't believe you?'

'Steve went through the motions, said he'd look into the fire reports, but I'm not holding my breath.'

'So what now?'

'*I* check it out and I think I might have some idea of where that fire was…' I froze.

Not six feet from me stood the young motorbike rider. His eyes were boring into me. It might have been the quality of his gaze that clinched it for me because something connected in my brain and recognition finally dawned. How could I not have seen it before? I must have been blind and stupid. He'd only been six then, but I knew without any doubt that he was Ben Lydeway, Alison's brother.

It was as if everyone else had faded away, and only Ben and I were in the room. I knew what he had come for: revenge for his sister's death. He blamed me for it. I should go and talk to him, but I couldn't move.

Then I saw him turn towards my painting of the international yachts moored up at Gunwharf Quays. His hand swept up and only then did I see he was holding a jar of something. There was a scream and then several screams, as he splashed some liquid from the jar on to my canvas and then on to another beside it. I felt as though someone had cemented my feet to the ground. People were scattering like startled starlings. They were shouting, rushing about. I registered a commotion out of the corner of my eye beside the door. I watched painting after painting being splattered with paint, and still couldn't move. Then two large men grabbed him, the jar fell to the floor and his body immediately went limp. But his head was erect and his eyes never left me.

He was led away without a struggle but even then he swivelled his head and gave me one last look. I guessed the whole episode could only have taken a matter of seconds but it seemed to have lasted for hours. My legs felt weak, my stomach was churning, my palms sweating and my heart was beating so fast that I could hardly breathe. People were beginning to crowd in on me, their mouths opening and shutting; their expressions concerned, but I heard nothing.

Then Jody's voice penetrated my senses. 'Fresh air is what you need.'

She led me through the kitchens and out of the fire exit at the back of the building where I sank down on a crate. Jody disappeared to fetch me a drink of water.

'Where's Faye?' I asked when she returned with a plastic beaker. I drank the icy cold water in one long draught.

'She's dealing with the press and the Minister. Who is that young man?'

'I don't know.'

Would I never be able to speak about Alison? I knew her death had been an accident but the fact that I couldn't remember where I was and what I had been doing at the time made me question myself. It was that uncertainty, the trauma of the incident, and the shame I felt over my breakdown that always kept me silent. The post mortem had found no bruises on her arms or upper body. Alison had been stuffed full of cocaine. They had tested me too, of course. I was clean. Drugs had never been my scene; I couldn't afford to lose control. Accidental death had been the verdict of the inquest but I had felt responsible. I *still* felt responsible. My row with her had led to her death whichever way I looked at it.

Would the police arrest Ben? Perhaps that was why he had vandalised my paintings. Did he want the police to re-open the investigation?

Jody's voice broke through my thoughts. 'He's probably an environmental protester. He knew the Minister would be here and thought he'd get himself in the newspapers.'

'Yes, that's probably it.' I pulled myself up. 'I'm sorry this had to happen tonight.'

'I don't think you should be the one apologising.'

Faye looked up as we walked back inside. I saw her frown before she sailed across to me with a tight smile on her pretty face. 'There you are, Adam.'

Jody said, 'I think I'd better go.'

'I need to talk to Martin,' I said, rather abruptly.

I left Faye to fend off guests and crossed to the despoiled images. There were three in total. Ben had splashed dark red paint across each of them. I snatched my head away. It was the colour of blood. I spent some time with Martin but can't recall what was said. My mind was many years away.

'Will you be able to salvage the paintings?' Faye asked, as a taxi whisked us out of the city home.

'Martin seems to think so.' I didn't really care. I knew that I wouldn't be able to touch them, not with that colour splattered all over them.

'Do you know who he was? ' Faye asked.

'No,' I lied.

'I wonder what made him do such a terrible thing,' she mused, and then answering her own question when I remained silent. 'Jealousy, I suppose, although the police said it could have been directed at the Minister, an environmental protest. How do you know that woman?'

'Jody?' I hoped my voice didn't betray my quickening heart beat. 'She's Rosie's neighbour.'

'Was she there when you rushed to Rosie's help after the break-in?'

'No.' I ignored her sneering tone.

'How did she get invited tonight?'

'I invited her Faye. OK?' I said hotly.

'No need to be so aggressive, Adam.'

The taxi pulled up outside the house. Faye followed me into the hall.

'You'll have to go down to the station in the morning to make a statement.'

I tensed. 'Why?'

'Because that man destroyed your paintings. That's wilful damage or malicious intent or something,' she snapped.

'I'm not pressing charges.'

'But, Adam –'

'I won't and that's the end of it.' *If only it were*.

'I don't understand. Why not?' Her voice was taut with anger.

I should have told her then about Alison. 'Pressing charges won't save my paintings. It won't undo what has happened here tonight. Let's forget about it.'

'You run away from everything, don't you, Adam?'

If only she knew about Jack! 'Drop it, Faye.'

'You're pathetic,' and she flounced out of the room.

I let out a breath. I should have told her. The moment had come and gone but I had remained silent. I couldn't get the words out. Soon I would have to. Soon Ben would tell the police everything and I'd have to explain what had happened to Alison not only to them but to Faye. I didn't think she was going to take the news very well.

I didn't expect to sleep. I lay perfectly still not wanting to wake Faye, staring into the blackness trying hard to remember more of the circumstances of Alison's death; they eluded me, as always. After a while I gave it up. It wasn't getting me anywhere. Angrily I pushed the past away and returned to Jack. I could hear Faye's gentle breathing beside me and, as the rain drummed against the windows I assembled the facts in my mind: I knew that the cancer had been caused by a fire, most probably on board a ship in the dockyard if Jack's choice of 'The Fighting *Temeraire*' meant anything, and that ship must have had some kind of chemical substance on it. The incident could have occurred on 4th July 1994. I still couldn't recall Jack mentioning anything about fighting a fire on board a ship, but then he had rarely talked about work when we were out sailing. I had to find out which ship and which substance. It sounded so simple. Maybe the fire reports would give me the answers on Monday. Until then I could do nothing but wait.

I turned over and pulled the bedclothes over me. Faye stirred. Tomorrow I would know if Ben had told the police about Alison's death.

CHAPTER 8

It was ten o'clock the next morning when they telephoned. I was polite but firm. They pressed me but I stuck to my decision. As I saw it, I had no option. The next call was from Steve Langton ten minutes later.

'What's this I hear about you not wanting to press charges?' he launched rather irritably. I didn't blame him.

'It's not worth it, Steve. They're only paintings; they can be cleaned.' A moment's silence in which I counted silently to five before Steve spoke.

'It's criminal damage. He could do it again.'

'Charging him and letting him go won't stop him, will it?'

'It might for a while,' he replied dubiously. 'I can't hold him. I've got a cell full of Christmas drunks and soccer hooligans.'

'Then let him go.' What if he comes here? I hoped he would. It was time for us to talk.

'His name's Ben Harrow.'

Harrow? Why not Lydeway? Had Alison's father died and her mother remarried? Perhaps Ben had taken his new father's name? Or had he changed it by deed poll? It didn't really matter what he was called, I knew it was Alison's younger brother. So he hadn't told the police about Alison. Or was Steve just trying me out?

Steve said, 'Do you know him?'

'No.' It was the truth after all. 'Did he say why he did it?'

'No. Martin says he didn't damage the building but he does want to claim off the insurance for the damage to your paintings. He'll need a crime number so the crime has to be logged. We have the culprit so we will need to charge him.'

'Then Martin can press charges.' I heard Steve sigh. 'How did he get in to the exhibition?'

'Said he was with the caterers, simply walked in.'

'Did he say where he lived?'

'He's staying at the White Sails Hotel, Southsea. We checked. He registered in the name of Ben Harrow a week ago. It's his real name according to his driving licence and passport. We ran a check through the computer: he's not got a criminal record and he's not claiming benefit.'

'Any joy with Jack's investigation?' I didn't expect anything but I thought I would ask anyway, if only to distract him from Ben Harrow.

'I sent an officer around to question the neighbours, but he got the three monkeys: see no evil, hear no evil, speak no evil. I'll apply to see the fire reports on Monday.'

'I've already done that. Brookfield is putting in a request for me.'

'Adam…'

'I need to know why Jack died, Steve.' Silence. I said, 'Did you know that Jack swapped his duty with another fire fighter called Ian?'

'Adam, leave it. You're barking up completely the wrong tree.'

Maybe I was but I didn't admit to it. His comment also made me remain silent about my idea of the fire in 1994 being in the dockyard. Red Watch was on nights tonight. I thought I might drop by and have a word with Ian.

After Faye had gone out shopping I headed for the White Sails Hotel. I steeled myself to meet Ben Lydeway's hatred and anger. I tried to rehearse what to say but I couldn't. What was there to say except that I was sorry his sister had died?

I parked in front of the hotel, which faced the rock gardens and the seafront, and removing my helmet walked up the four steps into a rather shabby reception where I interrupted a woman in her thirties in mid yawn. I asked for Ben Harrow.

'Room 14. First floor.'

I climbed the stairs feeling nervous. My heart was pounding. Ben had wanted a meeting; the demonstration in the art gallery, and his subsequent silence at the police station, were his calling card. If he hadn't spoken to the police then that could mean only one thing: he wanted to speak to me.

The door was ajar and the narrow corridor partly blocked by the chambermaid's trolley. I knocked and waited. Nothing. I tried again. Still nothing. A grey-haired woman carrying a white miniature poodle came out of a room further down the corridor and glanced at me.

'Ben, it's Adam Greene,' I said quietly. The woman tutted as if I'd said something obscene. As she passed me she made childish noises to her little white dog.

'Ben.' Still no answer. I pushed back the door half expecting to see the chambermaid inside but the room was empty. I crossed swiftly to a small en suite shower room but wherever Ben Lydeway was, it wasn't here. I made to leave when a silver-framed photograph on the bedside cabinet caught my eye. It drew me like a magnet. I lifted it and stared into Alison's laughing green eyes. My heart lurched. Her image had become clouded over the years, tainted by the memory of that accident. It was as if I was seeing her for the first time in years: the vibrant young woman and not the battered and bloodied body on the ground.

I stiffened. I had seen her on the ground then. I hadn't recalled that before and if that were so, I couldn't have been in that room pushing her. But perhaps I had run down the stairs after she had fallen? No, I was sure I had been on the pathway when she had fallen.

I replaced the photograph. The receptionist was on the telephone so I simply nodded at her and walked out intending to return later.

Perhaps Ben had gone for a walk to clear his head of the stench of incarceration, something I knew only too well. I crossed to the promenade and down on to the stones to the water's edge. To my left was the pier at the end of which were a couple of bedraggled fishermen huddled under layers of waterproof clothing and woolly hats staring into a gunmetal sea. It was damp and chill with hardly a soul about. The shops beckoned warmth, colour, life and light; offering the illusion of happiness that would dissipate the moment the tawdry wrapping paper was ripped off the presents that few people wanted and even fewer could afford.

My mobile rang. I didn't even bother to look at who was calling but answered it automatically.

'I thought I'd see how you are after yesterday.'

It was as if the sun had suddenly broken through the blanket greyness. My spirits lifted at the sound of Jody's voice and at the same time I felt a twinge of guilt that Faye had never had this effect on me, nor was likely ever to. Only Alison had made me feel something like this.

'I'm fine.'

She must have heard the hesitation in my voice. 'I haven't disturbed you painting.'

'No. I'm on the seafront. I needed a breath of fresh air.' I couldn't even tell her the truth.

'I'm sorry about your paintings,' she said gently.

'They're only paintings. It doesn't matter.'

A short silence then, 'Are the police going to charge him?'

'Not if I have anything to do with it. It's not worth it, Jody.'

'I'm sorry I dashed off like that. I didn't want to get in your wife's way.'

'That's fine.'

'You were going to tell me how you were getting on with your investigations.'

I told her about my ideas on 'The Fighting *Temeraire*'. 'I can check it out once I get the fire reports.'

'I'll ask around myself if you like. I'm based inside the dockyard. Someone might recall a fire here in 1994.'

'It's a long time ago.' I didn't hold out much hope of anyone remembering that far back. 'I don't think you should, Jody. It could be dangerous.'

'I'll be careful, I promise.'

I rode home feeling happier at having spoken to her but concerned that she could become a target herself. There was a message flashing on the answer machine. It was from Carol Rushmere. She had found her husband's scrapbooks and she said that I could collect them tomorrow evening if I liked. I did very much, I only wished I could go now.

Faye returned with her shopping and I retreated to the studio where I stared at the walls and canvases and played games on my computer. She called me when the evening meal was ready which we began to eat in silence only we didn't get very far before the doorbell rang.

'Who on earth can that be?' Faye said with irritation, rising to answer it but I beat her to it.

Standing on the threshold were two men: one tall and bony in his mid fifties, the other shorter and fatter in his mid thirties.

'Mr Greene? Adam Greene?' the younger of the two asked.

'Yes?' I replied warily.

'Detective Sergeant Wilcox and Detective Inspector Staples.' The younger man flashed his warrant card. 'Can we come in?'

I couldn't very well say no although I would have liked to. I felt a sliver of fear creep up my spine. I told myself they must have come about me not wanting to press charges against Ben. Would they send two officers of such high rank though? I doubted it. What did they want in that case? Could they possibly be here because Ben had told them I pushed Alison from that window?

'If it's about the incident in the art gallery last night,' I began, 'I've already said that I'm not pressing charges.'

'Who is it, Adam? Your dinner's getting cold.' Faye called out.

'It's the police,' I shouted back, then to the two policemen, 'You'd better come through.' I waved them into the lounge as Faye appeared in the hall.

'What do they want?' she mouthed. I shrugged. With a frown and a sigh she returned to the kitchen and I heard her put the dinner in the oven, as I followed the policemen into the lounge.

The sergeant sat on the sofa by the window but the inspector remained standing with his back to the fireplace. I saw his sharp, grey eyes scan the room. I perched on the chair directly opposite him. I did my best to appear relaxed, but I doubted if I was fooling anyone. Faye entered, and I quickly introduced her.

'We were just having dinner, inspector,' she said stiffly. 'Can't this wait?'

'I'm afraid not, Mrs Greene. There are some questions we'd like to ask your husband. We can go down to the station if it's more convenient.'

Christ! Ben *had* told them! They'd come to arrest me! I tried not to show fear but these men could scent it at a hundred yards. I wished Steve Langton were here. I tried to tell myself this was simply routine and it would soon be over, but I didn't believe it.

'I can answer any questions here,' I said abruptly. Faye flashed me a look and sat down in the chair next to me, across a small glass table.

The sergeant removed a notepad from his jacket pocket. 'I believe you know Ben Harrow, Mr Greene?'

My heart felt heavy with dread and a pulse throbbed in my head. I held the sergeant's eyes. 'No, I don't know Ben Harrow, but if you're asking me if I have met him then yes, I did. We both did,' I glanced at Faye, 'last night, at the art gallery.'

'And you haven't seen him since?'

'No.' My body was rigid with tension.

'You didn't call on him earlier today?'

I could feel Faye's eyes on me but didn't dare look at her. They knew I had been to the hotel. The receptionist and that woman with the poodle had seen me, but why had they told the police? Ben hadn't been there. Had he reported something stolen from his room?

Before I could answer Faye said, 'What is this all about, sergeant?'

The sergeant ignored her and kept his gaze on me.

I'd no option. 'Yes, I called on him at his hotel but he wasn't there.'

'Adam, why on earth did you do that?' Faye exclaimed.

'I wanted to know why he had damaged my paintings,' I replied as calmly as I could.

The sergeant spoke. 'What time was this, sir?'

'About ten-thirty. I went up to his room and knocked on his door. There was no answer.'

'You didn't go in?'

'Look, why are you asking me all these questions? *He* damaged my paintings, not the other way round. I'm not the criminal.' As I spoke, my mind was racing. Should I tell them I went inside and picked up Alison's photograph? Why were they interested?

'So you had a grudge against him?'

'Hardly a grudge. I was upset at my paintings but it's not the end of the world.'

'You didn't want to get your own back?' the inspector said. His tone was casual but his eyes were hard as granite.

'No.' Now I was puzzled. 'I went to talk to him.'

In the silence that followed I could hear my heart beating. It seemed so loud that I thought they must all hear it.

The sergeant spoke. 'You haven't answered my question, Mr Greene. Did you enter his room?'

I again had no option. 'Yes, I did. I called out to him in case he was in the shower and checked it when there was no answer. He wasn't there. I left.'

'Did you touch anything?'

I tensed. Why these questions? What had happened to Ben? Clearly something had and if that were so the police would take fingerprints. They would know. I said, forcing my voice to remain even, 'The doors obviously and I think I might have picked up a photograph frame.'

'Why would you do that, sir?'

I could feel Faye's eyes boring into me. 'I thought I recognised the woman in the picture.'

'And did you?'

Faye saved me. Her voice cold and firm. 'Inspector, I think you should tell us what has happened.'

The inspector looked at us, his hands clasped behind his narrow back. 'Ben Harrow was found dead in his hotel bedroom at two o'clock this afternoon. It is estimated he died some time between ten this morning and midday. We are treating his death as suspicious.'

His words sucked the breath from my body. Ben dead? How? Why? Who? My mind struggled to make sense of this.

Faye shot out of her seat. 'You can't possibly believe my husband has anything to do with that man's death. Adam wouldn't hurt anyone. This is preposterous.'

My mouth was dry, my head throbbing. Did this have anything to do with Jack's death? But how could it?

The sergeant said, rising, 'If you would like to accompany us to the station, sir, there are some further questions we would like to ask you.'

'You're arresting me?' I felt as though the room was spinning whilst I fought to keep calm.

'We'd just like to ask you some questions and take fingerprint and DNA samples. I hope you're going to co-operate, Mr Greene.'

The way he said it left me with little choice.

Faye said, 'I'll call Graham Johnson. He's a solicitor. Don't say anything until he arrives.'

'Faye, it's Sunday.'

'So? It's what he does for a living. Inspector you are making a *big* mistake.'

I looked at the inspector's face. He didn't think so.

CHAPTER 9

Graham Johnson arrived at the police station not long after me. We learnt from Sergeant Wilcox that Ben's room had been ransacked, which Wilcox accused me of doing in revenge for my paintings being destroyed. That also seemed to be the police's idea of my motive for killing Ben. I was glad Johnson was there. He made me stick to my story, the one I'd given the police at my house.

As the evening wore on, and the questioning grew more intense it took all my mental effort to concentrate and not let my mind flash back to the past and those other policemen in that other interview room. I held myself upright, my hands clasped tightly in my lap, the fingernails digging into the palms; I knew that if the two policemen saw this they'd probably interpret it as a sign of guilt.

Johnson remained icily cool. I drew some comfort from the fact that Wilcox was perspiring sitting in front of me and there were damp patches of sweat under his armpits.

Coffee had been brought in but I couldn't drink it. I was afraid my trembling hands would betray me. The tape whirred quietly in the corner recording everything that was said. I wondered if Steve Langton knew what was happening. Maybe he did and was not allowed to conduct the investigation being a personal friend.

'Why did you go there, Adam?' Inspector Staples leant back in his chair and examined his fingernails as if he was considering a manicure.

I'd lost count of how many times I'd said, 'Because I wanted to talk to him. I wanted to find out why he vandalised my paintings.'

Staples lunged forward, his face ugly with menace. Whatever he was going to say was interrupted by a knock at the door. A uniformed police officer appeared and whispered something in the inspector's ear. He frowned, scraped back his chair and for the benefit of the tape said, 'Interview suspended at twenty-three fifteen. Would you like more coffee?'

I shook my head.

The door closed behind the sergeant and the inspector, leaving a uniformed officer inside the room with us. Johnson unfolded his elongated frame from the hard chair and stretched.

'What do you think is going to happen now?' I felt exhausted.

'They'll either have to let you go or charge you. If they charge you, or think they have reasonable grounds to hold you, they can do so for up to fifteen hours before it goes before the superintendent who can hold you for a further twelve hours.'

A police cell. I didn't think I could handle that again.

'During that time they'll either try and make you confess or they'll try to get more evidence.'

My head came up. 'I didn't kill him.' And if I didn't who did and why?

'Whoever did, their timing is perfect.'

Johnson's words pulled me up sharply. I knew he meant the timing of Ben's death after the incident at the art gallery, but I interpreted his statement differently. What if this had something to do with Jack? How could it though? There was no connection between Ben and Jack, or the fire fighters who had died of cancer. No connection whatsoever, except…me.

Suddenly I felt cold. I had been making enquiries into Jack's death. I had almost been killed. Could someone be trying to frame me for Ben's death in order to get me to stop asking questions? Who would go to such extremes? It was crazy. And if I told Johnson he would think so too. The police would think me paranoid, and if they got hold of the psychiatrist's report after Alison's death they'd probably have enough to hold me.

Instinctively though, I knew I must be right. Poor bloody, innocent Ben. It made my blood boil. I was no longer afraid, I was very angry. Now I had Ben's death on my conscience and I had another reason to continue this quest. Only by getting to the truth could I make Ben's death mean something. But would I be allowed to? Only if the police let me go and they were hardly likely to do that.

That was where I was wrong.

The sergeant returned half an hour later, leaving the door open behind him as he walked in. 'Thank you for your co-operation, sir,' he said evenly. 'We'll be in touch if we need to speak to you again. Perhaps you wouldn't mind just making your statement to the officer here before you leave.'

'I can go?' I said startled. Even Johnson looked surprised.

'Yes, sir.'

I made my statement, refused a lift home from the police and accepted one from Johnson.

'It didn't look too good for you back there,' Johnson said, driving through Portsmouth's deserted streets.

Tell me about it, I thought. I peered through the windscreen into a mist-shrouded night examining recent events. Why had the police released me? Did they have new evidence that put me in the clear? Perhaps the police had changed their minds about Ben's death being suspicious. Even if they had I was still convinced that someone had killed him.

I knew that eventually the police would find out who Ben Harrow really was and then they'd make the connection with Alison. Would they return to question me? Maybe, but I didn't have time to worry about that now. I had to find out who had killed Jack. I'd already missed out talking to Ian tonight but he would be on duty again tomorrow night. And tomorrow I would talk to Sandy Ditton at the Maritime Museum.

Faye was waiting for me when I put the key in the lock and stepped inside the hall. She looked relieved to see me, but she didn't run to me with open arms. I followed her through to the kitchen giving her the gist of what had happened but I was too tired to go into much detail.

'I knew they'd made a mistake. How could anyone think you capable of murder, Adam? It's impossible.'

Is it? Although I didn't want to be accused of murder, it was Faye's tone that unsettled me. It reminded me too much of Simon's. Perhaps she hadn't forgiven me for not pressing charges against Ben.

'How do you know Graham Johnson?' I asked, a little later, as I stepped into the shower to wash the stench of that interview room off my skin.

'He was a client when I worked for the advertising agency in Portsmouth,' Faye called back. 'He's very good.'

'I'm glad he was there.'

I stepped out of the shower and towelled myself down walking through to the bedroom.

Faye was in bed. 'Will you be all right if I go into work tomorrow? We're very busy.'

'You don't have to wet-nurse me, Faye. I am capable of looking after myself.'

'I sometimes wonder that, Adam,' she said stiffly but I held her stare forcing her to look away.

I wondered if she would still have gone into work if I'd been locked away in a cell.

'I'm staying up in London all week,' she said, as I climbed into bed. 'You'll let me know when your father's funeral is, won't you?' Her voice was determined.

I didn't see any way I could prevent her from attending and now, strangely enough, I didn't much care.

I lay back and stared up at the ceiling. I was glad Faye wasn't going to be around. It left me with a clear field to pursue my enquiries, and it would be safer for her. I had no doubt that whoever was after me would try again. If Ben had been killed to frame me, or frighten me off, then who was to say they wouldn't try to harm

Faye, or Jody. I almost shot out of bed. I had to stop Jody from asking around. I wanted to call her then, but it was the early hours of the morning. Only another four and I could get up, another six and I could call her. My eyes swivelled to the clock beside me; I willed it onwards.

Faye shook me awake to say she was leaving. I wasn't sure what time I fell asleep; it seemed only minutes ago. I called Jody as soon as it was decently possible; even then it was barely eight o'clock. There was no answer. I left a message urging her not to make enquiries about the fire and to call me.

I showered, shaved and dressed. I called for Boudicca but she didn't come. I even rattled her dish but it didn't summon her. 'Stay out then,' I said, closing the door.

I felt agitated. Time was running out. Where had Ben gone yesterday? Had he been alone? Why had the police released me? Had someone else been seen entering the hotel with Ben?

He had been killed in his room and then the room ransacked to make it look as though I had done it. I wondered? Had Ben's killer been searching for a diary or notes that Ben had made about me and taken them? That would explain why the police had found no connection between Alison and me. If that was the case then why did the killer want to keep that secret? Surely it would have been better to have left it and further incriminated me in Ben's murder.

I couldn't wait around here all day waiting for something to happen. I telephoned Brookfield. He was on a course. Damn. I left an urgent message for him to call me. I needed those fire reports and I needed them now.

I listened to the news on the radio but there was nothing about Ben's death. Strange. I knew that what I was about to do might be foolish, but I didn't care. Ben's death had just upped the anti and I had to act.

There wasn't a policeman guarding the entrance to the White Sails Hotel and neither was there any blue and white scene of crime tape. It looked as though nothing untoward had happened there yesterday. I guessed the police must have got all the evidence and photographs they needed.

I crossed to the seafront and took up my position in the café. Here I could see in both directions: east and west. The woman with the poodle must exercise her dog at some stage and the best place for that exercise had to be along the seafront.

I waited a good hour before I saw her tottering towards me from the direction of Southsea Castle. I charged outside and began walking casually towards her. The poodle was on one of those stretchable leads and was sniffing around on the stones. I made for it.

'Lovely little dog,' I said, as it sniffed round my ankles. I ruffled his fur. 'What's his name?'

'Teaco,' the elderly lady said hesitantly, peering at me.

'Hello Teaco, little chap. I expect he can smell my cat.' I smiled.

'He hates cats.'

'He likes a walk though.' I looked directly at the dog's mistress who gave a little start of recognition.

'It's OK. Police,' I said authoritatively and quickly flashed my driving licence card at her, stuffing it away before she could peer more closely at it. 'I wanted a quick word with you. I'm undercover.' I wouldn't have thought myself capable of such deceit and daring but needs must…

'Is that why were at the hotel yesterday? Drugs was it? He looked like a drug addict.'

I nodded. Poor Ben. 'We're keeping it as low key as we can so that we can get the man behind the drug ring.'

'I thought as much,' she declared triumphantly. 'I told that other policeman about you. I didn't know who you were.'

'That's all right. You also told that other policeman about the man you saw with Ben Harrow, didn't you?' I waited with baited breath. Was I right?

'I heard them speaking.'

Yes! Was that why the police had let me go, they had another suspect. 'What were they talking about?'

'It was too muffled to hear. They didn't talk for long.'

No, I thought, the other man was busy killing Ben. 'Did you see this other man leave?'

'Not really. Only the back of him. I looked out of my window. He climbed into a dark blue van.'

The same colour van that Jody's landlady had seen outside Jack's house on the day of the funeral and break in. 'What was he like this man? Tall, short fat, thin?'

'Tallish. I couldn't really see.'

So, not much there. I was disappointed, though I hadn't really expected much. 'Did the receptionist see him? You must have talked about this.'

'The other policemen asked me all this,' she said irritably.

'I'm sorry but we have to check and double check. People don't always recall everything immediately after the incident. It can take a couple of days to remember something trivial that might actually be important.'

'There was some kind of commotion in the kitchen. Someone had left the tap on and flooded the place. She was called away to attend to it.'

Well-orchestrated then. I thanked her, ruffled the dog's head and with a plea for her to say nothing about our meeting that I doubted she would keep, let her go. I had learnt little, except Ben had probably been killed by a tallish man, but even that was unreliable.

I stopped off at the newsagents. There was a small paragraph on page three about Ben's death. I widened my eyes as I read, 'The police are not treating it as suspicious.' Why not? What about this other man? The article mentioned a suspected drugs overdose; the old lady had been right. The police hadn't told me how Ben had been killed even though I had asked. So, this wasn't a murder enquiry but either suicide or accidental death. Had I got this wrong? I made to close the newspaper when another news article on the opposite page caught my eye.

A fire at a residential nursing home on Hayling Island has claimed the life of an elderly resident. The fire at the Stella Hardlay Nursing Home was discovered in the early hours of Saturday morning by a member of staff. Three appliances from Havant and Hayling Island attended the fire and fire fighters helped the twenty-two residents to safety but one man had already been overcome with smoke. He has been named as Albert Honeyman. It is thought that the fire started in his room and was caused by an electrical fault.

Stella Hardlay not Stella Hardway!

I pulled out the postcard and went through the letters. Yes! I could get both names from Jack's letters – Stella Hardlay and Albert Honeyman. Had Jack called on this elderly man? My spine tingled. I knew he had. I didn't know *why* though, and there was only one way to find out. Hayling Island it had to be.

CHAPTER 10

The sea was grey and choppy as I crossed the bridge on to Hayling Island to the east of Portsmouth. I wondered if I should have called Rosie and told her who Stella Hardlay was, or rather what it was. I decided I would after I discovered exactly why Jack had been telephoning the place.

I swept into a gravel driveway that led up to a large Edwardian whitewashed house. I was surprised to find business as usual. This was explained by one of the carers who answered the door to me, a big boned young woman with a mass of marmalade-coloured hair and black eye make- up.

'The fire was at the back in the new extension. We've sealed it off and have had to double up on rooms. I can tell you the five residents we've had to move are not very happy. It's only until the end of the week but they don't like their routine being disturbed. They don't seem too upset over Mr Honeyman's death, but then he wasn't very popular, poor man.'

'It's him I've come to enquire about,' I said. 'A friend of mine contacted your nursing home a short while ago. He was a fire fighter, Jack Bartholomew, and—'

'You mean the man who was killed in the fire at the old Labour Club!' she exclaimed.

'You knew him?' I asked surprised. I hadn't expected instant recognition.

'I remember him because he was so friendly, and he came to see poor Mr Honeyman.'

My heart began to race. 'When was this?'

'About a month ago. Mr Honeyman told us not to let him in again if he called. I couldn't understand why, when he had no other visitors except one old man who looked like a tramp.'

What had Jack said to make Honeyman ban him from visiting again? And why had Honeyman died in a fire and now? Surely that was too much of a coincidence. I had to be on the right trail. I needed information about Honeyman and I needed it now.

'Can you tell me anything about him?'

'He was very temperamental. I hope that doesn't sound too disrespectful?'

I assured her it didn't with a smile and an encouraging nod. 'Did he ever talk about the past? What he did for a living?'

She was shaking her head. 'He didn't talk much at all, except to complain. You'd best speak to the matron, she could tell you more about him.'

Was my luck about to change? I hoped so.

After knocking briefly, the marmalade-haired girl pushed her head around a door and said, 'Mrs Davey, there's a man here would like to talk to you about Mr Honeyman.'

The middle-aged woman looked up from her desk with a scowl on her moonlike face. Hastily I stepped forward. 'I'm terribly sorry to intrude on you when you must have so much to do, but a friend of mine believes her late husband knew

Mr Honeyman. I wondered if you could tell me a little about him.'

Her expression softened. 'I thought you might be a journalist.'

She nodded her dismissal to the young woman and waved me into a seat opposite. She looked to me like a no-nonsense kind of woman in her sensible clothes and brogues. I hoped she'd give me some no-nonsense answers to my questions.

'This must be a terrible time for you,' I began. 'How did the fire start?'

'His electric blanket apparently. The fire investigations people have taken what remains away for further examination but it appears he fell asleep with it on and it short-circuited.'

I wouldn't have thought anyone would need an electric blanket here. It was stifling hot and I was beginning to sweat under my leather jacket.

She said, 'The owners will want a scapegoat of course; they always do. I might as well resign now only I'm not going to give them the pleasure.'

'Have any of Mr Honeyman's relatives been to see you?'

'He didn't have any.'

'Then who has he named as his next of kin?'

'His solicitor, Peter Goodman of Goodmans and Hopper in Portsmouth. I have, of course, informed them.'

'And is there nothing left belonging to Mr Honeyman, no photographs, diary?'

'No, the room is completed gutted.'

How convenient for the killer and inconvenient for me. I was convinced that whoever had killed Jack and Ben had also killed Honeyman.

'Perhaps you could tell me something about Mr Honeyman that might help Mrs Bartholomew. Her husband visited Mr Honeyman just before he was killed and she'd like to find out why'

Mrs Davey pulled off her gold-rimmed spectacles. 'I'm not sure there is anything to tell. He didn't mix very much.'

'According to the young lady who showed me in, Mr Honeyman didn't want to see Mr. Bartholomew again. Did they argue?'

'I don't know. But Mr Honeyman did seem very upset after Mr Bartholomew's visit.'

'Do you know why he wanted to see Mr Honeyman? It's a bit of a mystery to us.'

She shook her head. 'Then it will probably have

to remain one. I have no idea and I doubt Mr Honeyman would have confided in any of the other residents or staff.'

Another bloody dead end. 'What did Mr Honeyman do for a living?' I asked not really expecting her to provide the answer. I was growing used to disappointment

'He was in the merchant navy, a chief officer or mate as I think they are sometimes called.'

I sat up at that. Turner's painting immediately sprang to my mind. I had made the right connection: a fire on board a ship, not in the dockyard or a Royal Navy ship, but on a container ship, which meant the commercial port.

'Who did he work for?' I could trace the fire through his company. Judging by her expression though she obviously didn't want to tell me. Hastily I added, 'I'd like to contact them. It's possible that Mr Bartholomew was related to Mr Honeyman.' I could see that I wasn't convincing her.

'I'm sorry that information is confidential.'

He's dead, I felt like screaming at her. What harm can it do? 'It's important,' I urged.

'You'll have to contact his solicitor.'

Seeing that I would get nothing further from her I left as her telephone rang and headed back to Portsmouth. I tried Brookfield again, to be told he was still on his course. I left yet another message for him to call me urgently. Jody hadn't called me back either. I tried her again and got her answer machine. Damn! Where was she? I felt as though I was sitting on a time bomb. How long would it take before the police hauled me in again? Or how long before I was silenced like Jack, Ben and now poor old Mr Honeyman? The roll-call of dead was growing. The accidents becoming too numerous. This threat wasn't imaginary. Jack had known that and now so did I. I didn't want anything to happen to Jody.

I dropped into the solicitors and asked to see Mr Goodman, only to be told that I needed to make an appointment. This I duly did, with much irritation, for the next morning. I wasn't optimistic that he would give me the information I required so I decided to shortcut him – I called on Nigel Steep at the commercial port.

'It's good of you to spare me the time.'

Steep smiled, giving me the glint of a gold tooth. 'No trouble at all, Adam. I'm sorry about what happened at the exhibition. You must be devastated.'

'I hope they weren't the paintings you wanted to buy.'

'No, thankfully. Can they be cleaned?'

'I expect so. I've left Martin sorting that out. I've come because I'd like your help, Nigel.'

'Of course anything.'

'A friend of mine died recently, Jack Bartholomew. He was a fire fighter.'

'I read about that. Tragic business. I didn't realise you knew him. I'm sorry.'

I smiled my gratitude for the sympathy, which was genuinely given. 'I want to paint a ship on fire as a tribute to him and I think he may have attended a fire on board a ship here or in the dockyard, in 1994. Do you recall it?'

Steep shook his head. 'That would have been before my time. I've only been here five years. Can't the fire service help you?'

'They're checking their records, but I thought I'd just ask you.' I tried to hide my disappointment.

Steep said, 'You could try the Maritime and Coastguard Agency, they'll know, or the Marine Accident Investigations Board. They keep a database of reportable incidents.'

My spirits lifted. 'Do any of the ships that come in here carry hazardous cargos?'

'Some. The most dangerous we've had is lead but if there's a fire with that on board it gets ditched overboard very quickly, and that goes for other dangerous chemicals.'

I wondered what Jody would think of that and the possible danger to marine life. 'What would be the procedure if there was a fire?'

'The pilot would liaise with the Queen's Harbour Master and decide whether to take the ship out of the harbour and then put it alongside a navy facility if possible, so that they could fight the fire.'

'So if I were to paint a container ship on fire in the port that wouldn't be realistic?'

Steep hesitated. 'It's possible but unlikely. A fire at sea would be better, with a tugboat or a navy boat squirting water jets on to it. Fire fighters would probably fight it from a safe distance after making sure the crew were off.'

'And that would be big news?'

'Oh yes.'

I had found nothing like that in the local newspaper. It had to be something else but I was so convinced I was right.

Outside I got the number of the Marine Accident Investigations Board and put in a call to them. A lady said she would check it out for me and e-mail me any details. The Maritime and Coastguard Agency said they would check and could I call back tomorrow?

I grabbed a late lunch by the Hard where the tourists milled around the steel warship, HMS *Warrior*, and then made for the Maritime Museum hoping that Sandy Ditton would remember a fire in 1994.

'Can't say I do,' he said, after I had given him my story about the painting.

We stepped out of the museum. A stiff damp wind rolled off the sea bringing with it the taste of salt and the smell of mud. Behind us was Nelson's flagship, HMS *Victory*, with flags flying from its three tall masts.

Ditton took a packet of cigarettes from his jacket pocket and offered me one. I declined. Even before he spoke there was something about the thin, auburn-haired man in his late fifties that irritated me. Perhaps it was his air of self-importance.

I hadn't forgotten that this man was on the watch in 1994 and could be the next cancer victim, like Brookfield. If Ditton had remembered, and it had been that easy, then Jack would have spoken to him and got to the truth quicker and certainly before he died. Ditton would also probably have met with an accident, which made me think that perhaps all those connected with whatever incident had prompted the cancer were dead. Honeyman could have been the last link, or rather the last but one: there was still me. Then it dawned on me. If Jack couldn't recall the fire himself that had caused the cancer, but had had to interview men like Honeyman to trace it, then it couldn't have been very memorable. It also meant that the others on the watch at that time were unlikely to recall it. This was a waste of time.

'1994…That was the year Tony Blair took over the Labour Party.'

'Was it?' I replied disinterestedly, itching to get away.

'Not so you'd notice any difference between his lot and the Tories. The Labour party stole the middle ground right under the Tories' noses. I stood for Parliament once, against Bill Bransbury. He was Conservative then. I didn't get elected, glad I didn't now, the state the party's in, but old Bransbury's done well for himself since he crossed the floor. Tony rewarded him of course, Minister for the Environment, Energy and Waste.'

Hastily I interrupted trying to salvage something from the interview. 'Did you ever keep a diary or scrapbook?'

'Only of my political career. You're welcome to look at that.'

'No thanks,' I said rather hurriedly and saw Ditton frown at my ungraciousness.

'I'd better be getting back.' He pinched out his cigarette with his forefinger and thumb and returned the butt to the packet.

'If anything occurs to you perhaps you'd give me call.' I handed him a card

'Be pleased to.'

I was unable to shake off the impression that I had made a mistake in involving Ditton. There was nothing to actively dislike about the man but I was left with a bad taste in my mouth. There was something not quite genuine about him, but that could be because of the size of the man's ego. When he had stepped out of the museum he had the air of a man who owned it rather than worked in it, still that was no crime.

Every avenue I explored became a cul de sac. Where the devil was Brookfield with those fire reports?

A voice hailed me and I looked up to see Jody waving at me. Relief and pleasure flooded through me as I hurried towards her.

'Where have you been? I've been trying to contact you all day.'

Her smile quickly vanished to be replaced by an anxious expression. 'What's wrong?'

'We can't talk here.'

'I'll meet you in the café in Action Stations in five minutes. Just let me dump these.'

Only now did I see the large plastic bag full of barnacles and other sea encrustations in her hand, and that her hair was plastered to her small head. A very large red and navy sailing jacket swamped her, reaching almost to her knees.

'OK.'

I waited impatiently in the mezzanine café, my eyes scouring the entrance for her. A couple of minutes later she arrived, minus the sailing jacket and plastic bag.

'Didn't you get my message?'

'I've been out on a harbour launch visiting the site where the *Mary Rose* was found and collecting sea specimens. What's happened?'

I told her. She looked worried. I didn't blame her. I was worried. 'I don't want you asking around, Jody. In fact, I don't want you having anything more to do with this.'

She let out a long breath. In the silence that fell between us I could hear the sounds of the interactive attractions, the voice-overs of the videos and the whirring of the simulated rides in a Lynx helicopter.

Her eyes locked mine for a moment. She made to speak then seemed to change her mind.

'I want you to promise not to do anything. This isn't your problem.'

'It's not yours either, Adam,' she said quietly.

'I owe it to Jack.' I hadn't told her that I knew Ben. I hadn't told her about Alison.

'Jack's dead. He won't know. If you stop now you'll be safe.'

I stared at her. There was something in her eyes and in her voice that bothered me. I couldn't say what? I couldn't pin it down. Was it more than concern? It sounded almost like a warning, but why should she warn *me* off? She looked away and scraped back her chair.

'I must be going.'

'Jody…?'

'Yes?'

'I can't stop. I have to go on.'

She smiled sadly. 'I thought you might say that.'

I watched her walk away. At the entrance she turned. As I made my way to Carol Rushmere's I couldn't get Jody's expression and her tone of voice out of my mind. Neither could I forget her words. She hadn't promised not to ask around. Why should she still want to help? This wasn't her fight. This wasn't anything to do with her. Jack had only been a neighbour. Or had he?

I rode slowly over the speed humps in the wet, cold December evening trying to shake off the feeling that there was more to Jody Piers than she had led me to believe, and more perhaps to her relationship with Jack. I didn't much like those thoughts so I tried to shove them away. They persisted, seeping into me like the rain.

Carol Rushmere handed me a plastic carrier bag containing three scrapbooks. I only needed the one that covered 1994 but I didn't tell her that.

Boudicca was waiting for me when I reached home. I left her gobbling down her dinner as if I'd starved her for a week and took the carrier bag through to the lounge where I poured myself a large whisky and withdrew the three soft-covered books. I opened the first one, which spanned the period from 1990 to 1995. The first page contained two press cuttings of fires, *Woman Rescued from Kitchen Blaze* and *Blaze Home hit by Smoke Damage*. There were also some photographs of firemen dressed in women's clothes at a pensioners' Christmas party. The date was 1990. I recognised Jack dressed in a woman's wig, stockings and suspenders with clown-like make-up on his face. A fleeting smiled tugged at the corners of my mouth.

The following pages chartered Vic Rushmere's fire service career: a blaze at the old bus depot at Eastney before it was pulled down to build houses, an armed siege, a car crash, a warehouse blaze, and a fire wrecked garage. 1994 and more fires, an explosion in a block of flats, floods at the small village of Finchdean, more charity fundraising events, a naval exercise that involved a mock blaze on board a ship in the dockyard and a workman freed from a trench that had collapsed on him. Then came a series of press cuttings taken on bonfire night, a blaze in a hotel on the seafront, a house fire... but I had gone too far, I was now into 1995.

I flicked through the remaining pages, but could only see more of the same. Could it be that mock ship blaze? I turned back the page. It was the right year but wrong date. It was in April and not July. Perhaps the date on the postcard, 4th July, had nothing to do with the actual date of the fire but had just been used by Jack to draw my attention to the quotation?

Was there something on board that ship that had triggered the cancer? But it would only have been an exercise and a Royal Navy one rather than merchant navy. Honeyman wouldn't have been involved in that.

I sat back with a sigh and sipped my whisky, feeling disheartened. Boudicca strolled in, glanced at me and seeing I was too restless for her to sit on, plumped for the rug in front of the fireplace. She didn't like the leather chairs, which I think was the reason why Faye had bought them.

Surely it was mad of me to continue with this. If I stopped now perhaps they'd leave me alone. But they hadn't left poor Ben Lydeway alone. Jody's words came back to me: *if you stop now you'll be safe*. I didn't owe those fire fighters anything; surely I could walk away? But I couldn't.

No matter how many warnings I had I was determined to get to the truth.

The phone rang making me jump. It was Simon.

'Cremation's on Thursday 12.30pm. The wake's at the house, Harriet's organising it. Are you coming?'

'Yes, I'll be there.' I rang off and almost instantly my phone rang again. This time it was Brookfield. At last.

'Adam, I'm sorry but the incident reports you want aren't available. They've been taken away for data entry; the system is being computerised.'

How bloody convenient, I thought, trying to stem my disappointment. Of course it was a lie and if it was a lie then was it Brookfield who was lying or was some power higher up pulling the strings? If that were so then this thing was bigger than even I had guessed at.

I stared down at the scrapbook. Someone was going to a great deal of trouble to keep a secret, and one that had cost lives and was still costing them. I knew I couldn't give up. Even if it meant my death, I had to continue. I was surprised to find that the thought exhilarated me rather than frightened or depressed me.

'Here's to you, Jack,' I said quietly, tossing back the remainder of my drink. I thought I almost heard him answer.

CHAPTER 11

It was almost 8.30am the next morning when I called at the fire station.

'Ian's gone sick. His doctor's put him on anti depressants and signed him off for a fortnight,' Motcombe, the gangly fireman, said in answer to my enquiry.

Blast. 'Could you give me his address; I'd like to talk to him about Jack.'

'Not sure that's a good idea, Adam. He's pretty cut up.'

'Perhaps it will help him to talk,' I suggested.

Motcombe didn't seem convinced.

'What do you want to know? Perhaps I or one of the others can help.'

I didn't blame him for being protective towards one of his colleague. I knew from Jack that there was a strong mutual bond of support between the fire fighters. 'Why did Jack swap with Ian?'

'No particular reason. We do that sometimes. Why do you want to know?'

How much should I tell him? It wasn't that I didn't trust him, just that I thought the fewer people who knew about my investigations the fewer I would put in danger. I erred on the side of caution. 'I'm just trying to make some sense of Jack's death, I suppose.'

Motcombe looked sympathetic. 'It's hard I know. There is no reason for it, Adam. It was just one of those things.'

'You're right of course.' After a moment I said more brightly, 'There is another reason for my visit; it's to do with my painting. I wondered if you could show me around the station so I can get a feel for the place?'

'Of course.'

We ended the tour in the appliance room. The wide doors that led on to the rear yard were open.

The watch was getting ready to change over. My eyes caught sight of a board to my right. 'What's that?'

'The manning board.'

I crossed to look at the coloured tallies hanging on the small hooks, each tally was engraved with the name of a fire fighter.

Motcombe explained. 'The board shows which watch is on duty, the tallies are colour co-ordinated to match the watch: red for Red Watch, green for Green Watch and so on. The red tallies are on the manning board at the moment because we're on duty but they'll shortly be changing over to Green Watch for the day duty.'

At the top of each of the four columns on the board was a set of initials. 'What do those mean?'

'Wrl means water tender ladder, Wrt is the water tender, TL stands for turntable ladder and SEU stands for special equipment unit. The fire fighter's tally is then hung on the relevant hook to indicate which appliance he or she has been assigned to.'

'So where would Jack's tally have been on the day he died?'

'Here, to show he was on the water tender ladder, riding in the back, wearing breathing apparatus.' Motcombe indicated the appropriate spot on the board.

'And it would have been there after he swapped with Ian?'

'Yes. Initially the manning sheet would have shown Jack driving the water tender and Ian wearing breathing apparatus. I seem to remember that they swapped after Dave read out the duty roster that morning and then the tallies were changed over.'

So, if they knew where to look, someone could easily have slipped into the station when these doors were opened and seen that Jack was on the water tender and wearing breathing apparatus, which meant he'd be first into a fire.

I thanked Motcombe and headed for my interview with Honeyman's solicitor. He told me nothing. I left his office fuming as his brittle voice echoed in my head: 'That is confidential, Mr Greene.' He'd uttered it after my every question. Damn him. I hoped all his clients would sue him.

I called Steve Langton to tell him what Brookfield had said about the fire reports not being available.

'Snap,' he replied. 'I got the same response.'

So it wasn't Brookfield who was lying, unless of course he had also lied to the police.

Steve said, 'I was going to call you.'

'You've got something to tell me about the investigation?' I felt my heartbeat quicken.

'I'll meet you in the Wayside Café in ten minutes. Do you know it?'

I did. It was only about a half mile from the solicitors.

I arrived before Steve and took my coffee to a table the furthest away from the window. Then I got to thinking. Perhaps Steve was going to tell me something about Ben's death, which had nothing to do with Jack's investigation. Had the police found new evidence that connected me to it? Had the old lady reported me? If she had, I reasoned, Steve would hardly ask to meet me, and in a café, unless he wanted to warn me. I'd find out soon enough.

I was shocked to see how tired and worried he looked. There was a deep frown line creasing his forehead that hadn't been there last week and his shoulders seemed more hunched than usual as if the heavy workload had suddenly become a strain for him. Steve had always seemed to thrive on it before.

'You're working too hard,' I said after he sat down with his coffee.

'Try telling the Super that!'

He stared at me with an expression that made me feel uncomfortable. It was as if he was trying to see inside my mind.

'I wasn't involved in Ben's death,' I said quietly.

'I know.'

I breathed a sigh of relief. He believed me. 'How did he die, Steve? Inspector Staples was reluctant to tell me he thought I already knew.'

'I shouldn't be telling you this. Drugs overdose.'

'That's what the newspaper article said.'

'Yes, but what it didn't say was that Ben Harrow wasn't a regular user.'

It took a moment for his words to sink in. 'You're saying someone administered it?'

'I'll get crucified if anyone finds out I've told you this.'

'You haven't,' I said quickly, wondering why he *was* telling me.

'He was shot full of heroin and there was nothing to indicate he had even used the substance before.'

'Not a nice way to kill yourself, which means it must have been...'

'He could have got some on the street, didn't know how much to use being new to it…'

'Yeah and my middle name is Rembrandt. Apart from me was there anyone else seen with Ben? Where did he go that morning? Who did he meet? The old lady with the poodle said she heard him talking to someone.'

'You've spoken to her? For God's sake, Adam!'

'I think he was killed to set me up. No, listen. I've been asking questions about Jack's death –'

'Stop there. You don't know what you're getting yourself into.'

Steve studied me. The tune of a familiar Christmas song floated through the steamy atmosphere of the café. After a moment he sighed heavily, shifted in his seat and ran a hand through his hair before speaking. 'Do you still think there was something funny about that break-in at Jack's?'

Eagerly I said, 'Yes, and there's more. I've been to the fire station and –'

Steve held his hand up to staunch me. 'Whatever it is, Adam, forget it.'

'I can't do that,' I replied flatly.

'You might after you hear what I've got to say. This morning I got hauled up in front of the

Super. He wanted to know all about you and our relationship.'

A chill ran down my spine. I was beginning to understand why Steve looked so worried.

'He ordered me to drop both cases. In precisely twenty minutes time I'm off for a short secondment to Basingstoke.'

'Did he say why?' I asked, my heart and mind racing.

'No. It's clear though someone wants me out of the way for a while. Whoever it is doesn't want me mixing with you and they don't want me, or you, poking around and asking questions about Jack's death.'

I knew it. If ever I wanted confirmation here it was. 'Then Jack's death wasn't an accident.'

Steve urged, 'Adam, you don't want to know about it and neither do I. I've got a wife and three boys to support.'

'I can't leave it, not now.'

'You must. If I'm being pushed away that can only mean one thing, another agency is involved: National Crime Squad, Special Branch, MI5? Take your pick.'

'Why would they be involved?'

Steve leant forward and lowered his voice even

though there was no one near us in the café and the music was loud enough to drown out our conversation. 'Because whatever Jack was investigating must have national ramifications.'

'You mean a scandal involving someone high up in government?' Why did William Bransbury automatically spring to my mind?

'Either that or a national operation involving government secrets. It could be terrorism, international fraud, drugs…'

'People have died, Steve.' I said quietly.

'And you could be next in line if you're not careful,' he snapped.

'You're not suggesting that one of these government agencies would kill me!' I said incredulously.

'Why not? It's happened before. It could have happened to Jack.' Steve sat back.

I thought for a moment. Then, 'Can you find out which agency is involved?'

'No I bloody can't.' Steve shouted. Then more quietly, 'Go on holiday, Adam. Go sailing, forget it.'

But I couldn't do that. Maybe Steve saw the determination in my face because he frowned at me and said, 'I didn't know you were so bloody stubborn.'

And scared, I thought. I said, 'Someone has to pay for the deaths.'

'It might just be you.'

'Get off to Basingstoke, Steve.' I was on my own.

I returned home and went straight to switch on the computer. While I waited for it to load I looked around my studio: the canvasses, the brushes, the rags, the palettes and pots of paint, they were all still here as they had always been, but it wasn't the same. Nothing was the same anymore. And yet, despite being half scared to death, I didn't want to go back to how my life had been less than a month ago – with one exception: I wished Jack were still alive.

I watched the spam programme on the e-mail roll down until I had one message left in my inbox out of the fifty-five that had come through. It was the one I'd hoped for but it didn't contain the information I wanted. The Marine Accident Investigations Board reported no ship fire in 1994 in or around Portsmouth or anywhere in the Solent. I felt the disappointment keenly. I had been so convinced I was right. I telephoned the Maritime and Coastguard Agency and after a short while, which to me seemed like an age, they confirmed the same. Dead end. So if it wasn't on a ship the fire had to be either where Honeyman had lived or stayed. Could it be that hotel?

I pulled out Vic Rushmere's scrapbook and re-read the report on the hotel fire but it revealed nothing and it seemed highly unlikely that anything inside the hotel could have caused cancer. Perhaps Sam Frensham could enlighten me I thought with little hope. If Jack, Des Brookfield, and Sandy Ditton couldn't recall it what hope had I of Sam Frensham doing so?

Rosie had given me the location of Sam's hotel as being just outside Stow on the Wold, in the Cotswolds. I found the details of it on the Internet and arranged to see him that afternoon. It would only take me an hour and a half to get there on the bike.

It was just gone three when I rode up the long gravel driveway to the old Manor House, which looked old enough to have accommodated King Charles I. I was shown into an office just behind the main reception by Sam who proved to be a jovial man, in his mid fifties with a balding head and twinkling blue eyes. I liked him immediately.

'You said on the telephone this is about Jack Bartholomew.' He waved me to a seat by a modern desk, which was in sharp contrast to the rest of the hotel. On the desk sat the latest state of the art computer. 'Good man, Jack, one of the best.' His blue eyes looked sad for a moment. 'I remember him coming on watch as a probationer. He was slightly older than the usual recruit because of his navy service. Joined when he was in his late twenties. I think I was in my late thirties then. There was about ten years between us. Good fireman. Loved the job. Never wanted promotion though he was good enough and clever enough to get it, but sitting behind a desk wouldn't have suited Jack. He was a real action man.' He smiled as the memories flooded back. Then he shook his head. 'Bloody shame. I don't suppose they've caught the little bastards who put that gas cylinder inside the building?'

'It wasn't kids and it wasn't an accident.'

Sam looked surprised.

'It's my belief that gas cylinder was placed there deliberately and the building flashed up in order to kill Jack.' Sam was eyeing me as if I'd gone mad. 'It's a long story.' I wasn't sure if I should take him into my confidence and if so how much

I should tell him. I liked his easy manner, his genuine concern, his kind words about Jack, his unquestioning hospitality at a very busy time of year, and I could tell that his staff liked him by their manner towards him.

Sam said, 'If there's anything I can do to help you only have to ask. Jack was my buddy. He and Rosie stayed here a few times.'

I told him as much as I dared, leaving out the attempt on my life, Ben's death and my arrest. At times Sam stared at me with an incredulous expression on his face, at others he scowled; several times he sat back and ran a hand over his bald head, seemed about to say something, then stopped himself.

Finally he exhaled and said, 'So you reckon this cancer was caused by something hazardous in a fire we attended in 1994?'

I nodded.

'OK, so let's work this out.' Sam rose and began to pace his office. 'Five men dead, that would mean that two appliances went to the fire.'

'Two?'

'We'll say the water tender was riding the officer in charge, a driver, a BA controller and two men in breathing apparatus, for example, Vic and Scott. The second appliance, the water tender ladder, would have been carrying a driver and possibly three fire fighters wearing BA. That could have been Duggie, Tony and Jack. Only those men wearing breathing apparatus would have gone into the fire, making it the five. The BA controller stays outside, the drivers operate the pumps, and the officer in charge usually runs around like a headless chicken.' He gave a brief smile.

'No one else would be at risk then?'

'No…unless the first pump was riding one more fire fighter wearing breathing apparatus.'

Sam looked worried. I didn't blame him. He pulled a photograph from the wall behind his desk. 'That leaves, me, Dave Caton, Sandy Ditton, Des Brookfield, Colin Woodhall, Brian Clackton and Stuart Hallington.'

'And, according to Brookfield, possibly two other fire fighters who were on secondment.'

'Brookfield knows about the cancer?'

'No.'

'And you say you can't see the fire reports?'

'No. Can you can recall a fire on board a ship in 1994?'

'Let me think. I left the brigade in 1996, bought

my first guest house, which I sold in 2000 to buy this place. Best thing I ever did. So it would have been two years before I left. I was forty-four then. I resigned,' he explained. 'Could have stayed on until retirement age at fifty-five but didn't want to. My mother died leaving me her house and some money and Helen and I thought we'd give this business a go. Always wanted to. Sorry I'm rambling, but I am thinking.' He stared down at the photograph. '1994? I thought, at Jack's funeral you know, how many of us from the old watch were gone. Lucky Brian's still alive...for now.' He turned back to face me. 'No, I can't recall any sort of fire that might have contained chemicals and especially on board a ship. That would have stuck in my mind. '

Disappointment washed over me. I felt as though Sam was my last hope and now I saw it slip through my fingers like grains of sand. 'It was the year Tony Blair became leader of the Labour Party so Sandy Ditton tells me,' I said rather cynically and bitterly.

'Was it now. Not that interested in politics but Sandy always was. More interested in that than being a fire fighter. Stood for Parliament once. 1994. Tony Blair. Hang on.' The gleam in his eyes made my heart leap. His telephone rang and I had to curb my impatience.

I crossed to the photographs as Frensham handled an enquiry about some bed linen. They were much like Jack's, taken on exercises, at charity functions and visits to schools. There was a watch photograph with the men posed in front of an appliance. Why had one of Jack's photographs been missing? Could it have provided a clue to my investigations? Had there been anything in that empty frame in the first place?

'Sorry about that,' Frensham said as he finished his call. 'Now where were we? Yes, there *was* a fire on board a ship, of course. But the ship wasn't at sea; it was tied up in the port. That's what threw me until you said that about Tony Blair.'

I didn't have a clue how that could have made a difference and I didn't much care as long as Sam Frensham could help me. Was I at last about to get a break? I resumed my seat and sat forward eagerly.

'I was pump man,' Frensham continued, evidently with relief. 'If it is *that* fire then there *were* two pumps. I was on the second one with Jack and Tony. They went in wearing breathing apparatus but the first pump had almost extinguished it.'

I leaned across the desk. 'Can you recall what was on fire?'

Frensham screwed up his face in concentration but finally shook his head. 'No, sorry. I didn't go on board. Thank goodness,' he added with feeling. 'Neither Jack nor the others ever said anything about it. It was a simple fire quickly extinguished. I do remember though that the ship wasn't loaded. You think it might have been that?'

'I don't suppose you remember the name of the ship or the date?' I asked without any real hope, wondering if he would confirm it was 4th July.

Frensham shook his head. 'No. The only reason I do remember it is because you triggered my memory, Tony Blair, politics. I saw that MP at the Port. William Bransbury, MP for Portsmouth East. The one who was Tory and went over to New Labour. You see that was my constituency then and I voted for him and not Ditton.' He grinned.

'What was Bransbury doing there?' Steve's words came back to me. Was someone protecting him?

'I don't know.'

'It was daytime then?'

'Yes, must have been.'

'Hot or cold? Summer or winter?'

Sam thought for a while. 'Summer.'

So it could have been on the 4th July.

Sam said, 'I'm really sorry I can't be of more help.'

'You've already been a great help. Look, if you do remember anything more please let me know, won't you?'

Frensham waved away my gratitude. 'If I can help Jack, or any of the others, you only have to ask. You will tell me how you get on, won't you? Come and stay for a couple of nights on the house, bring your wife.'

'That's really very kind of you,' I said shaking his hand, thinking I'd rather bring Jody. My last image of her flashed through my mind. She stirred more than desire in me but this time that longing was tainted with unease. There was something about our last exchange in the dockyard that troubled me. I couldn't say what though.

As soon as I reached home I looked Bransbury up on the Internet. He was born in 1958, the same year as Simon, educated at the local grammar school and then took a degree in Science at Oxford. Would Simon know him? It was possible; they must have been at Oxford together though not necessarily on the same course. He was married with two children and lived just outside of Portsmouth. His interests were football, tennis and surprise, surprise, the environment! There was no information on him holding any surgeries but I could e-mail him through the House of Commons website. I decided to telephone first and ask for his office. On the third attempt I got through to his secretary. I asked if he could check Mr Bransbury's movements in 1994, which involved a visit to the Portsmouth ferry port. I got a frosty reception and was told to put my request in writing with an explanation of why I needed such information. I e-mailed him, wondering if I would ever receive a reply.

There had to be some kind of record of MPs' engagements but though I searched the Internet I couldn't find one. I found snippets of his visits since becoming a minister in 2005 with details of speeches and some photographs but nothing for when he had been an MP in 1994. Then I recalled what Ditton had told me. Bransbury had been a Conservative MP in 1994. I found articles about him crossing the floor in 1997.

The local conservative party might be able to help me with that visit to the port in 1994 if I needed it. It could be pure coincidence. There was someone else I could ask first though.

I telephoned Nigel Steep, hoping he would still be in his office. It was gone six. He was.

'I need a couple of favours,' I said. 'Can you find out for me which shipping lines used the port in the summer of 1994?'

'Of course, and the other favour?'

'William Bransbury, the Government minister, visited the port in July 1994. Can you find out when he was there and what he was doing?'

'That might be harder to answer. I'll get back to you tomorrow.'

I spent some time staring at Jack's postcard and the message taken from the Gideons New Testament and Psalms trying to see if I could squeeze anything further from it.

His mouth is full of …deceit and fraud, he murder the innocent.

That implied that Jack had discovered the identity of the person who had placed something dangerous on that boat. Could he be referring to Bransbury?

I re-read the postcard:

Look after 'Rosie' for me, Adam. You're an accomplished artist and a good friend. Happy Sailing!
Best Jack
4 July 1994

I couldn't get Bransbury's name from the letters on the postcard. I pinned it back on the board above my computer and desk and stepped back inside the house from my studio. As soon as I did I knew something was wrong. I strained my ears but could hear only the gentle whirr of the central heating boiler. Despite the silence I knew someone was inside the house. My mind rapidly replayed my conversation with Steve. He'd been sent to warn me off. I had ignored the warning. Had our conversation been bugged? Steve hadn't succeeded so now I had to be told in stronger terms. Men had died because of this secret. Now it was my turn.

A shiver ran down my spine. My chest tightened. I struggled to get my breath. My hands began to tremble.

Run away, said the coward's voice inside me. I wouldn't. I crept forwards through the kitchen into the hall. Empty. Something creaked behind me. Someone was there. I made to turn round when something struck me on the side of the head.

It was pitch dark when I regained consciousness. Boudicca was meowing like mad and pushing up against my shoulder. I tried to move but a sharp pain shot through my head. I must have drifted off again. The next time I awoke my head was still hurting but not quite so fiercely. Slowly, testing the pain threshold with each movement, I propped myself up. As I grew acclimatised to the pain I began to be aware of my surroundings. I was in the hall.

The phone rang. I let it. Whoever had attacked me had let me live, why? I could so easily have been finished off and my death made to look like an accident, a house fire perhaps, or a fall down the stairs?

I shuddered and hauled myself up. Wincing and clutching my head I dragged myself into the kitchen, almost blindly, wondering if I would ever get full vision back. When I removed my hand there was blood on it. I rinsed it under the tap and then poured myself a glass of water and drank it thirstily. I felt sick and dizzy and knew that I really ought to go to hospital but I didn't want to, besides I didn't have the energy and I couldn't ride the bike, not in this condition.

Staggering back to the lounge I sprawled myself on the sofa where again I drifted into unconsciousness. I woke once and managed to reach the downstairs cloakroom before being violently sick. Then hauling myself back to the lounge I threw myself once more on to the sofa. If they came for me now I'd be an easy target. The pain in my head was so intense that I couldn't give a damn if they did.

When I woke some time later there was a chink of light coming through the bay window. I raised myself up on an elbow; the pain wasn't nearly so severe and I could see. There was no double vision. My mouth felt like someone had stuffed it full of sandpaper and my hand rasped over my unshaven chin. But I was alive and in one piece and clearly it was morning.

I clawed my way up the stairs and shaved carefully, staring at my haggard face in the mirror hardly recognising the man who stared back at me. Then I stood under the shower until I felt almost human again.

'Who were they, Boudicca?'

She meowed at me as if to say how the hell should I know, tucked her tail around her body and laid her head down on the soft duvet of the bed.

I coped with breakfast, and slowly and miraculously my brain began to function. Yet, no matter how well I exercised it, it could not come up with a reason for why I had been allowed to live. Maybe it had been a sheer fluke. Maybe I had a thicker skull than the attacker had anticipated.

I crossed to the studio. Before I reached it I could see that the door was open. Cautiously I moved forward and pushed my fingertips against it, my heart knocking against my ribs and steeling myself for another attack or sight of the intruder.

Slowly the door swung open and I stepped inside. But there was no intruder, only the chaos of my wrecked studio. I picked my way through the debris to my desk and stared up at my notice board. Jack's photograph, the postcard and the message from the Gideons New Testament and Psalms had gone. Someone was wiping the trail clean. Next time it would be me.

CHAPTER 12

Despite my pounding head I made my way to Rosie's. I couldn't see anyone following me but that didn't mean to say they weren't. If Steve was right and it was MI5 or Special Branch then I guessed I wouldn't spot them, just as I hadn't heard or seen anyone enter the house. They'd be too well trained for that. I wasn't sure how safe it was to stay in the house. Would they try again when they saw I was alive and still determined to get to the truth? I guessed so.

Rosie looked so bereft when she answered the

door to me that it filled me with an even greater resolve to find the bastards who had killed Jack and who were having a pretty good go at finishing me off. I gave her a hug and felt myself connect with Jack.

'Sally's here,' Rosie said.

At first I thought she meant her daughter but my sluggish brain finally recalled that her daughter was called Sarah, not Sally. I entered the lounge to find Jack's colleague from Red Watch perched on one of the chairs. I was pleased to see her. If Rosie couldn't help me perhaps Sally could.

I said to Rosie, 'I came to ask if you have Ian's telephone number and address.'

'No, I don't, sorry.'

'I've got his number,' Sally volunteered, as I hoped she would. I smiled my thanks. As I copied it from her mobile onto mine she said, 'Why do you want it?'

'I want to talk to him about Jack.'

She thought for a moment then shrugged. 'Perhaps it will help him.'

'Do you know where he lives?'

'St James's Road, Locks Heath but don't ask me the number. I only know the house. It's a colour-washed bungalow in yellow. Poor Ian. He feels so responsible.' Sally flashed Rosie a look.

'It wasn't his fault,' Rosie said. 'It was just one of those things.'

I didn't comment on that. I addressed Sally, 'What was Jack like on that day? Was he acting differently in any way?'

Rosie flashed me a worried look.

Sally said, 'He seemed a bit quieter than usual.'

'Were you there when he swapped with Ian?'

'No. I was making a coffee for DO Brookfield.'

Brookfield hadn't mentioned he'd been on the station the day Jack had been killed. Then a terrible thought struck me. Brookfield could have seen that tally board. Brookfield could have been lying about those missing fire reports. Brookfield could have killed Jack! No, that was ridiculous. I couldn't believe it. But perhaps he had passed the information on to someone who wasn't so squeamish when it came to committing murder.

'What did Brookfield want?' I asked lightly.

'He came to see the station officer about something, I don't know what.'

Outside I rang Ian's number and got his wife.

'He went out early this morning for a walk and

he's not returned. I don't know when he'll be back,' she said after I had briefly explained that I'd like to talk to him. She sounded tense, and I could hear a child crying in the background.

'I'll call again later.'

I returned home, scouring the street for anyone loitering or sitting in parked cars. No one. Cautiously I let myself in listening for sounds, only Boudicca padded down the stairs to greet me.

My mobile rang making me jump. It was Nigel Steep. 'No joy on what the minister was doing at the port, Adam, but I have got the names of the shipping lines.'

There was only one that was no longer using Portsmouth; Greys of London; all the others were local firms and mainly imported fruit.

I powered up my laptop, connected to the Internet and looked up Greys. They were a privately owned company, which had begun trading in the late 1960s with a number of small coasters and barges supplying Portsmouth and the Isle of Wight. Since then they had expanded to mini bulk carriers, and had grown their fleet of container ships to forty-six carrying grains, fertilisers, steel, and minerals. They could also carry hazardous goods such as explosives and ammunition.

I called them from my mobile phone, knowing from the films I'd watched that landlines could be tapped, and gave them the story that Albert Honeyman was my uncle. I managed to get an appointment with someone from human resources for Friday. Tomorrow was Thursday, and my father's funeral. I decided I would stay in London overnight, but not at father's house. I also decided I would say nothing to Faye.

I left a whole lot of food out for Boudicca, which she'd probably gobble up by the end of the day, and told her to go next door if she got hungry. Then throwing some clothes and toiletries into my sailing bag and collecting my lap top computer, I climbed on to my bike and headed for Hayling Island, checking that no one was following me. When I climbed on board my boat moored in the marina at the northern end of the island I didn't think anyone had.

I telephoned Ian again but he still hadn't returned home. His wife sounded frantic. I didn't blame her. I was beginning to get worried myself. Had Ian gone walk-about to try and escape his depression? Had someone followed, or lured him away, because they didn't want me finding out why Jack had swapped duties with him? Or had Ian disappeared because he was partly to blame for leading Jack to his death? Had someone paid Ian to swap with Jack on that fateful Wednesday? Is that why he was so cut up? Was it more than just sorrow? Was it a huge burden of guilt that young Ian carried? If so, I didn't rate his poor wife's chance of being reunited with her husband.

Steve called me. I was surprised. 'It's Special Branch,' he said abruptly.

I gripped the phone tightly. 'Do you know why?'

'I've already put my neck on the line for you, Adam.'

'I know and I'm grateful.'

'I'd rather have you alive.'

'You don't mean they'd silence me permanently.' I rubbed the side of my head.

'Of course not, but if they're involved it means that whoever they are after is a hell of lot nastier and wouldn't hesitate to kill you if they had to.'

'Good job I've taken your advice then, Steve.'

'You'll let things alone?' The relief in his voice was palpable.

'Yes,' I lied.

'Thank God for that. Go away for a few days.'

'I will. Thanks, Steve.'

I rang off.

I had done a fair bit of sailing in the dark but in the summer rather than winter. Still that couldn't be helped now. I wasn't going to risk staying in the marina. That call to my mobile could be traced. Special Branch would know where I was. I wanted to believe Steve when he said they wouldn't kill me but I wasn't going to take any chances. And if they knew maybe whoever they were after would also know my whereabouts.

I hadn't asked Steve how he had found out it was Special Branch because I wasn't sure he would tell me the truth. As I motored slowly out of Northney Marina I couldn't quite believe that he had discovered it for himself. Someone had told him. Just like they had told him to make the call. They wanted to know where I was. Tonight I would elude them but tomorrow was a very different matter. They would be able to find me easily because tomorrow I would be at my father's funeral in London.

The cremation was short. No lingering speeches, no memorial sermons. I had Simon to thank for that. During it my mind had wandered back to my conversation with Ian's wife that morning. He hadn't returned home. She'd reported his disappearance to the police. Would they connect it with Jack's death? I guessed only in the fact that Ian was depressed about it and felt guilty.

I glanced around the faded lounge of my father's Belgravia house, trying to stifle a yawn after a fitful night's sleep on the boat. I had picked up a buoy in the Emsworth channel and returned to the marina in the morning to shower and collect my motorbike. Perhaps I had over reacted because there was no one lurking around the marina that looked suspicious and, as far as I could tell, no one had followed me to London.

I had checked my phone for messages before the service. Jody had called me. She sounded anxious. My heart tugged at the sound of her voice enquiring how I was and what I was doing. It took a great deal of effort to resist calling her back. I desperately wanted to. I told myself it would only put her in danger. If Special Branch could locate where I was calling from then maybe they could locate whom I was calling?

'It's Adam, isn't it?'

I spun round to find a tall, elegantly dressed man with a leonine sweep of grey hair sleeked back from a distinguished looking face. He looked familiar but I couldn't place him.

'Tim Davenham. I was at Oxford with Simon.'

'Of course.' I took his hand and returned the pressure.

'Simon tells me you're an artist.'

'Yes.'

'And a successful one by all accounts. Your father would have been proud.'

I doubt it, I thought, scrutinising Davenham for signs of irony. He showed none but I had a feeling he was sneering at me. Maybe it was my inferiority complex.

Across the shabby, crowded room Faye was talking to Simon. She laughed at something he said, Simon smiled. He was at his most charming. They'd hit it off immediately.

'She's very attractive,' Davenham went on, following my gaze. 'But Simon always did have an eye for a pretty girl.'

Before I could reply he'd excused himself. I watched him join them. I couldn't recall Davenham that well from Simon's past. I had only a vague recollection of a clever, handsome man who attracted women like a magnet. Simon hadn't done too badly for himself either I seemed to remember.

I looked at Faye as though seeing her for the first time. She had managed to get herself her a little black dress that hugged her shapely but slender figure and showed off her long legs, clad in black stockings. She was at her most seductive in the hope, I suspected, of wheedling some of father's inheritance from Simon. Judging by Simon's reaction to her I didn't think she'd have much difficulty. I saw the point of Davenham's remarks. He had wanted to rub my face in it. A month ago I might have reacted. A year ago I would have been upset, devastated even, but now? I didn't really care. When had I stopped loving Faye?

'They seem to be getting on well, don't they?'

I turned to find Harriet beside me. Her shapeless figure was clothed in a drab black dress. Her limp blonde hair hung around a lined face with skin that was dull and eyes that were sad. It was as if she had long ago forgotten how to smile. It made me think of the last time I'd laughed and again I thought of Alison. She'd had that capacity to make the world seem bright. Nothing could dampen her wild spirit or her optimism. To her life had been living on the crest of the wave and never rolling on to the shore. Jody made me feel like that.

'I'm sorry about the will, Adam,' Harriet said, breaking through my thoughts. 'I told Simon he should share it with you, or at least see that you're all right but...' She took a nervous sip from her glass.

'Don't worry,' I said dismissively, meaning it. I hadn't yet had the chance to slip into my father's study and extract my file.

Davenham looked across at me. Simon and Faye followed his glance.

'I didn't expect to see so many people,' I said, feeling angry and averting my eyes.

'The obituaries in *The Daily Telegraph* and *The Times* account for that,' Harriet replied. 'I received a lot of calls from former colleagues and members of the Royal Society of Chemistry as a result. Your father was quite famous.'

Yes, I supposed he was. In the 1950s Lawrence Greene had discovered a compound that had had huge commercial ramifications in the manufacture of processed foodstuffs. This house and the ones in Cornwall and Wales had been bought on the proceeds of it and Simon and I educated at an expensive public school that I loathed and at Oxford, where my life had changed. Now only this house was left. What had happened to the proceeds of the other properties? Were they in the coffers waiting for Simon to inherit?

'You'll sell the house?' I said.

'Yes, Simon's already had it valued but we can't really do anything until after probate. I'm sure Simon would let you have something; there are some good paintings here.'

Harriet was right, there were some good paintings, but I didn't want anything to remind me of this place or my father. My mother's paintings had all been sold a long time ago.

'Do you know if Simon's been through the rest of Father's papers yet?'

'No, you'll have to ask him. I don't think he's had much time what with the business. It's all been rather hectic.'

'Of course.' The American deal. Had Simon clinched it?

The sound of Faye's laughter drew my attention for a moment, but when I looked back at Harriet her unguarded expression took me by surprise. I wondered how many affairs my brother had conducted during their marriage.

I turned back to look at Faye as Harriet saw her, another of Simon's conquests. Faye was clearly flirting with him and enjoying it but she was in control, or so I told myself. I thought of Stewart, her boss, and all the clients she entertained. I thought of Graham Johnson, the solicitor, I had no reason to think that Faye had been unfaithful, but in my gut I knew she had been.

'How are the children?' I turned my back on Faye. For a moment the light stole into Harriet's eyes.

'William's doing very well at boarding school, but I miss him so much.'

'And Daisy? Didn't Simon say she was away at school too?'

'If that's what you want to call it.'

I was shocked by the bitterness in her voice. She saw that she had given herself away and blushed furiously whilst trying to bury her face in her glass.

'You don't like her school?' I coaxed.

'No. She was better off living at home with us

and going to our local school but Simon disagreed and you know Simon he always gets his way,' she said bitterly.

'What does Daisy think?' I saw her startled expression.

'Daisy doesn't think; well, not like you and me.'

'Of course she's only a child.'

She looked puzzled. 'You don't know, do you? Simon hasn't told you. He wouldn't. That's why he's sent her away to that special school. He doesn't want to be reminded of imperfection. Daisy has what they call special needs. She's handicapped.'

'I had no idea, Harriet. I'm sorry.'

'Yes, so is Simon.'

Her words wrenched at my heart. 'Perhaps the money will help you have Daisy home again,' I said gently, but Harriet was shaking her head.

'It's not about money, is it, Adam? Not where Daisy's concerned.'

No. It wasn't. Harriet was called away. It was getting late and already dark. Time to get that file. I doubted if Faye would even notice if I slipped away. Before I could reach the study, however, a tiny woman in her sixties, with grey waved hair, a shrewd, sharp face, lively eyes and a cockney accent waylaid me.

'You must be the other brother. Adam, isn't it? I'm Mrs Withers, your father's housekeeper. I'm sorry about your Dad. He was a fine man.'

I simply nodded.

'Difficult time for you, and Dr Greene, especially him being so fond of his father.'

That was news to me. I mumbled something but she didn't seem to hear. Mrs Withers charged on regardless.

'Not a week has gone past these last six months without Dr Greene looking in and often staying overnight.'

My ears pricked up. Simon had never done a single thing in his life out of kindness so why start now? But I knew the reason. *Money.*

'I know you and he didn't hit it off,' she swept on. 'Not that Dr Greene ever said much about it and Dr Greene, sorry, your father that is, never so much as spoke of you. I didn't know there was another son until your brother told me after your father's stroke. But I expect it was difficult for you to come and see him, being estranged so to speak.' She sighed heavily. 'Still, he wouldn't have known who you were even if you had come, not these last few months anyway.'

'What did you say?' This was news to me. Why hadn't Simon told me that father had been unwell for some time? But then what right had I to that information? I had chosen to cut myself off from my family.

'Sad, isn't it, when you think of the fine brain he had. Makes you wonder. Life can be so cruel, don't you agree?'

'I'm not sure I understand you.'

'Dementia,' she nodded sagely, as if an expert on the topic. 'Poor man didn't know who I was half the time, let alone your brother. Patience of a saint that man. Used to sit with him in his study for hours. I'm sorry your dad's gone, but in a way it was a mercy wasn't it, being taken so quickly. He would have gone into a home soon and they just eat away at the money, don't they?'

Oh, yes, don't they, I thought. And Simon wouldn't want that being the sole benefactor of Father's considerable will. When had my father cut me out of his will? After Alison and Oxford? After my breakdown? After I had walked out of this house fifteen years go? Or was it more recent, such as in the last six months during which time Simon had worked on father to change his will.

Damn. I should have stayed longer the first time I'd returned to the house with Simon. I could have seen then when the will was dated and I could have extracted my file.

I pushed against the study door and stepped inside. Stretching out my right hand I flicked on the overhead light and gazed around. My eyes fell on the battered mahogany desk in front of the french windows. I recalled standing before it as a boy, trembling with fear. I remembered that day I had been in here when I shouldn't have been. I can't remember why, but I had sneaked in and then been trapped as my mother and father had entered. Hiding behind the curtains I had heard him humiliate her with his harsh words and cruel, sarcastic tongue. There were too many ghosts here and in this house and the sooner I got that file, the sooner I could say goodbye to the place forever.

The room was clammy. I couldn't quite steel myself to sit at Father's desk so instead leant over to search the drawers. They weren't locked but there was nothing of any interest in them except a key, which I removed and crossed to the four-drawer grey and scratched filing cabinet in the far corner of the room. The key opened it and methodically I went through its contents. It contained the usual papers, household insurance and receipts. Then, in the bottom drawer, I found what I had been looking for, a buff-coloured folder that bore the name of the clinic I'd attended after my breakdown. If Simon had got this far then he hadn't thought the contents of sufficient interest to remove.

I extracted the folder and locked it in the box on the back of my motorbike. Then returning to the house I found Faye.

'I'm heading home now,' I lied.

'All right.' She didn't protest or plead with me to stay.

'Are you staying in town tonight?'

'You know I am.'

'I'll see you tomorrow night.'

Maybe Faye would find out tonight what had happened to me at Oxford, if not from Davenham then from Simon. I didn't care. I knew the time was fast approaching when it would come into the open anyway, but not, I hoped, before I found out who had killed Jack and Ben Lydeway. I was pinning a great deal on this meeting with Greys tomorrow.

I booked myself into a bed and breakfast not

far from Victoria Station. It was small, cheap and rather nondescript but it was clean. I threw my bag on the bed, along with my helmet and gauntlets and returned to the bike. I lifted open the box and stared inside it horrified. It was empty. The file had gone.

Chapter 13

I rode slowly along the Embankment. The Thames looked sludgy and lethargic, gunmetal grey in the dull morning with only the odd splash of colour caused by the riverboats. Across the river I could see the London Eye revolving slowly. Weaving my way through the stop go traffic I thought about that missing file, much as I had thought about it for most of the night. Who had taken it and when? I knew why, to use it against me.

The police may have released me in connection

with Ben's death but that didn't mean they wouldn't arrest me if they felt they had more evidence. I wasn't absolutely sure what the psychiatrist reports would say about me, having never read them, I only wish I had, but I guessed it would make for interesting reading: my self recriminations at Alison's death, my lack of memory. The police could argue that I killed Ben whilst suffering from a black-out.

Who had taken it? Had someone been watching the house, seen me come out with a file, guessed that its contents might be useful and then stolen it? That seemed unlikely. Even if whoever it was knew there was a file documenting my breakdown after Alison's death how would they have known my father had it and that it would be the one I was carrying. If the police, or Special Branch, wanted information on me surely they could get it simply by obtaining a warrant and taking it from the clinic?

It had to be someone inside the house: one of the guests at the wake and the most likely candidate was Simon. Perhaps Simon had seen me take the file and had been afraid it contained something that would ruin his chances of inheriting Father's estate? Or perhaps he'd taken it to discredit or, worse, blackmail me if I ever decided to contest the will? But if that were so then Simon would have taken it before now. He'd had ample opportunity.

My head was aching with so many thoughts whirring around inside it as I wound my way past the church of St Clement Danes and the old nursery rhyme popped into my head, *'Oranges and lemons say the bells of St Clement's.'* When I reached the bit about the chopper coming to chop off my head, I shivered and looked behind me. I couldn't see anyone following me but I had the feeling they were. Someone knew every step I took.

I moved through Fleet Street and up Ludgate Hill. The traffic was heavier than I had anticipated. As I halted at the traffic lights I watched a flock of starlings rise above the great dome of St Paul's Cathedral. I envied them their freedom. The responsibility of finishing Jack's quest weighed heavily on my shoulders. But I had to continue with it, no matter where it took me.

At last I turned into Monument Street and then Lower Thames Street where I found Greys

Shipping. After waiting ten minutes in the spacious reception area, where I studied rather splendid models of ships owned by Greys, I was shown up in a lift to an office on the third floor by a young, very bored-looking girl who did nothing but chew gum. The woman who greeted me in a large office was very different. She was confident and friendly, with hair the colour of a blackbird's wing and startlingly blue eyes.

'I would like to trace some of my uncle's ex-colleagues to let them know about his death and the funeral arrangements,' I said, repeating the lie I'd told her secretary on the telephone in order to get the appointment. I felt uncomfortable at deceiving her but I had no choice.

'Of course.' She picked up a file from the table in front of her and resting it on her lap she opened it and extracted a piece of paper. 'I've prepared a list of the personnel who sailed with your uncle during his time with the company from 1990 to 1994.'

I was surprised at her efficiency, but I shouldn't have been after seeing her office. It was so orderly that I felt slightly scruffy sitting in it with my black leather jacket, leggings and heavy boots.

I quickly scanned the names on the list. There

were only a half a dozen. 'I thought there would be more than this?'

She smiled. 'There are never that many crew members on a container ship. There is so much technology now, and on the size of ship that Mr Honeyman sailed the maximum crew would only have been six. Of course since your uncle sailed with us, sadly some of the crew have died.'

And I'd liked to know from what. I glanced down at the list and saw, with interest, that one of the men lived less than a mile from Albert Honeyman's nursing home. It was the Master, Captain Frank Rutland.

'There is something else that you might be able to help me with, Miss Rogers. Do you know if there was ever a fire on board one of the ships in which my uncle was serving?'

She looked surprised at the question but she didn't probe me about it. She said, 'I don't think so but I can check for you.' She crossed to her desk, her heels clicking on the wooden floor, and began to tap into her computer.

I waited with baited breath glimpsing only briefly at the paintings on the wall of sailing barges on the Thames in the 19th century. I willed her to find something. Surely I hadn't come all this way for nothing. No file and no fire.

It appeared I had.

'There's no record of any fire on any of our ships, Mr Greene.'

I felt more than disappointed, I felt desperate. 'Could there have been a fire that wasn't reported?' I asked hopefully. I registered her surprise.

'I doubt it. A fire on board a ship is very serious; even if it wasn't carrying any cargo the captain would still have to report it.'

How could there be nothing? I had to be right, but I didn't think Miss Rogers was lying. I had wasted my time and my hopes. In the process I had possibly put myself in danger of being arrested for Ben's death when whoever had stolen my file decided to give it to the police.

I thanked her with little enthusiasm. There was only one more place to go and that was to Captain Frank Rutland. If he couldn't help me I really didn't know what to do next.

The Christmas traffic was a nightmare. As I weaved my way through Convent Garden I thought of Faye. I had never been to her office and I wasn't about to go there now. If she knew I had stayed in London, it would only give her more ammunition about moving here. Perhaps if I did I might save my marriage. Was it a sacrifice worth making?

I pulled up at the lights and gazed across the crowded street. It was as if my thoughts had conjured her up. There she was and she wasn't alone. Faye threw back her head and laughed at something Simon said. He smiled down at her. I could see so much in that smile. I watched them duck into a restaurant, the traffic began to move, a car hooted angrily at me and I let in the clutch and pulled away.

It was getting dark by the time I reached Hayling Island. At the sign to the boatyard I indicated left and turned into a road that gave way to a track. It wound its way past two Nissen huts, left over from the Second World War, until it opened up into a boatyard. A handful of boats were resting up for the winter in front of the boatsheds on my right and there were a long row of masts stacked above each other on their side.

I asked one of the workmen where I could find Frank Rutland's boat, and eventually, three people later, managed to track it down. It was lying at the end of the last pontoon.

It was exposed here with nothing ahead but the mud of low tide and the sea. Beyond, across Chichester Harbour, was the flat landscape of Thorney Island, once used by the Royal Air Force in the war and where the army still had a base. Lights blinked at me in the distance. The wind cut across the channel. The day had grown colder; even the seagulls seemed to have fallen silent as if in anticipation of a storm; I could see them squatting on their narrow legs in the mud facing into the southwest wind. I felt the first lean spits of rain.

I made my way down the rickety pontoon glancing at the variety of boats until I came to Rutland's. It was older than most of the others, a classic though, a Hillyard 8 ton 30-footer. She was a beauty, or rather had been in her day. It was clear from her neglected air and rotting timbers that those days had long gone, but with a little care and a lot of money she would still be sailing when many modern boats had been consigned to the scrap heap. The hull needed cleaning but she still looked sound.

I called out whilst running my eye over the weathered mahogany deck. Hillyards were solid boats built to last and this one looked as though it had been around for the last forty years or more. It was resting on the mud of low tide. It looked much lived in and used with its off-white sails reefed down and looped around the boom. A rusting, but still operational bicycle was propped up on the foredeck along with a battered striped deckchair of the kind that used to be seen along the promenade in Southsea occupied by old ladies in crimpolene suits and gents with their trousers rolled up and knotted hankies on their heads.

I called again but still got no reply. I groaned. I hadn't come all this way just to find the guy out. Perhaps Rutland didn't want to see anyone? But if Rutland had gone out then perhaps I could wait for his return.

I climbed on board. The hatchway was open and, calling out, I began to climb below when suddenly I drew up, staring in disbelief and horror at the sight that greeted me. Lying in front of me was a skeletal man of about seventy, with grey frizzled hair and a beard, dressed in a pair of old navy jogging pants and a dirty T-shirt. There was blood around his nose and mouth, his lips were blue and his scrawny neck was livid with bruises where someone had squeezed the breath from him.

Suddenly, pressing on my eyeballs was the memory of another dead body. I felt a rush of air and heard a thump, a sickening crack; eyes were staring wide and blood was trickling from the smashed skull until it reached my foot. Seeing Rutland had brought back every detail of Alison's death. Now I remembered it exactly. I had rowed with Alison and then had left the party. As I was walking away she had fallen out of the window and landed right in front of me. I could see the blue dress she was wearing: it had rumpled up to her knees; one sandal was still on, her other foot was bare. I saw the expression on her face and the blood trickling from her mouth.

Forget Alison. Forget what had happened fifteen years ago, I urged myself. Think of now. I had to get away. I stumbled up the gangway trying to get my breath; my legs trembled so much that they could barely carry me. Christ, Rutland murdered! Who the hell...

I glanced nervously over my shoulder. They had killed Ben Lydeway, Honeyman and now Rutland. Whoever had killed these men could be watching me now.

I climbed on to the bike and roared away. I knew I should have stayed and reported it to the police but that would mean my chances of solving Jack's murder would be nil.

I glanced back over my shoulder as I reached the main road. There was no one following me. The next time the attack on me might be fatal. Either that, or the police would come to ask me questions. Miss Rogers would confirm she had given me Rutland's name and address, the three men in the boatyard I asked directions from would confirm I was seeking Rutland and that, with Ben's murder, would give them enough to detain me.

If I explained, surely they would believe me? Would they though? Even if they believed me, and they knew me to be innocent, someone more powerful didn't want me on the loose sniffing around and discovering a secret so big that it had already resulted in the deaths of three men, four, if you counted Jack. I had no alibi, a possible motive and suspicious behaviour. My heart was heavy as I climbed on board my boat. Danger was closing in on me. My enquiries were going nowhere.

'For Christ sake, Jack,' I cried, 'Give me a break, a sign, anything. I have to get to the truth and soon before it disappears for ever.'

I found a bottle of whisky and the hot liquid slid down my throat, warming me.

When would Rutland's body be discovered? Tonight? Tomorrow? Next week? I might have believed next week or next month if it wasn't for the fact I was convinced someone wanted to frame me for his murder just as they had tried to frame me for Ben's. An anonymous telephone call to the police would be all that it would take. The police would need to examine the body and then question people and that all took time. They would test for DNA on Rutland's body – it wouldn't match mine – but I might have left a trace of DNA by simply being on the boat, and I would certainly have left my fingerprints. The police would match these with the ones they'd already taken from me after Ben's murder and bingo!

I guessed I had a couple of day's grace, maybe even a few, *if* I was very lucky. In that time I had to get to the truth. But with Rutland dead how could I?

I stretched out on the bunk and let my mind trawl back through the events of the last couple of weeks. I came to no new conclusions, so I thought back to before Jack was killed. Had there been anything that he'd done or said to me that could give me any clues? Apart from that last vague conversation, when he had told me he was being followed, there was nothing. I thought about the message on the postcard. Whoever had taken the postcard hadn't erased the message from my mind:

Look after 'Rosie' for me, Adam. You're an accomplished artist and a good friend. Happy Sailing!
Best Jack
4 July 1994

Jack's message had led me to the Gideons New Testament and Psalms and to a possible fire on 4th July 1994, which Sam Frensham had recalled but Greys hadn't documented. Could Sam have been mistaken? No. I thought it far more likely that Rutland, and possibly Honeyman, had hushed it up because whatever had been on fire on board their ship had contained something hazardous. *Happy Sailing!*

'Here's to you Jack. I shall think of you every time I sail in her.' I lifted my whisky to toast him when I paused. *Happy Sailing!* Why had Jack given the word 'sailing' a capital S and an exclamation mark…This had been Jack's boat. Had he…Suddenly my heart was pounding. Could Jack have possibly got on board? Had Jack kept or found a spare key? Had he left a message for me here? Had he hidden his computer disks and diary on *Tide Mark*?

I leapt up and with the water slapping against the sides of the yacht, hardly daring to hope, I began my search.

CHAPTER 14

I found the computer disk stowed away inside the sail cover under one of the bunks. There was no label on it, but I didn't need any label to know what it might contain.

I powered up my laptop, thanking the heavens that I had brought it with me. I inserted the disk. The rain was hammering on the boat and the wind howling around it. My pulse was racing. Was I at last about to get to the truth?

It was written as a diary. With my quickening heartbeat I began to read Jack's account of his investigations.

31 October
It's too much of a coincidence that Vic, Scott, Duggie, Tony and now me should all contract cancer; it must have been from a job we'd all been on. Before we had the new flash hoods our ears had been exposed to fire. It was the only way we could tell how hot the fire was and if we should get out whilst we still could. Those hoods were abolished late in 1994, so the fire that has caused our cancer must have been before that – but how long before it?

There were more entries as Jack doggedly traced fires involving chemicals, and eliminated them matching the incident with the manning reports. I skipped through the entries until 7th November. Eureka! There it was.

I've finally managed to trace the fire. It has to be this one. We all attended it. It was a small fire on board the *Mary Jane*; she was tied up in port. It was 4 July 1994. The incident report was filed by Des Brookfield.

It figured. Brookfield had done well for himself over the years, big house, expensive motor yacht, exotic holidays abroad and kids in private education. Perhaps he didn't know the full extent of what had been on that ship but he had been paid to keep silent. *His mouth is full of ...deceit and fraud, he murder the innocent.* This was who Jack meant. Brookfield had lied about those fire reports being sent away for computerisation. I couldn't believe that Brookfield had killed Jack; he must have told the killer that Jack had swapped duty with Ian. Perhaps Brookfield had even commanded Ian to swap. I read on.

> The Third Officer was on watch, he was the only person onboard at the time and he called us out, but by the time we got there he'd almost extinguished the fire. The ship's captain was Frank Rutland and the chief officer Albert Honeyman.

I skimmed down the rest of Jack's diary until I reached the following entry.

> There was nothing to indicate that there was any hazardous cargo on board, in fact there was no cargo, not in the hold at least. The fire had been below in a packing case. But what was in that case? There was nothing to warn us that its contents might be lethal. But it must have been. It has to be that fire, nothing else matches up. I need to talk to Honeyman and I've traced him to

the Stella Hardlay Nursing Home, quite by
accident. I was on secondment to Havant when
we had a call-out. Someone was stuck in the lift
and there was Honeyman. He didn't want to say
anything at first but I pushed him, it didn't take
much. Perhaps he wanted to end his days with a
clear conscience? He told me he'd always had his
suspicions over what they had been carrying
especially when the third officer had died of
cancer not long after the fire.

I read on as Jack documented that Honeyman
believed they were carrying illegal cargo on each
trip but didn't think it was his business to raise it
with the captain. All he knew was that it didn't
go through any forwarding agency and wasn't
packaged like the rest of the cargo, in a container.
It came on board separately, ready packed, and
Rutland always oversaw its lading.

Jack managed to track down Rutland on 1st
December.

Called on Rutland. He lives onboard his boat on
Hayling. I could see as soon as I arrived that he
knew why I'd come. He said he wondered how
long it would take for someone to find out. He
confirmed that he had been well paid to carry
the small cargo on each trip. Someone would

arrange to take it off when the ship docked at Calais. All Rutland had to do was transport it no questions asked. Shortly after the fire, the cargo stopped coming aboard. I asked Rutland who had paid him, he said he didn't know. He was lying. I asked where the cargo had come from but all he would say was a laboratory on Salisbury Plain. It made me think of the RAF base there, but when I asked Rutland he would neither confirm nor deny it. Will call on them tomorrow. I'm almost there, near the truth. I'm being followed though and I am sure that my telephone has been tapped. I will store this on disk and leave it on my old boat.

Jack's next message drew me up with a sharp intake of breath.

Adam, if you're reading this now then I'm probably dead. I've written you a coded message, on a postcard, which I shall post tomorrow. I know you don't like puzzles but I have every confidence you'll work it out. I'm sorry to have burdened you with this, but there is no one else I can trust. I've enjoyed every minute of our friendship and I know I can rely on you to take care of my darling Rosie. How much you tell her about this I will leave to you. Here's hoping you get to the truth and expose the bastard who is behind this. If you don't, and you stumble on this disk in months, or even years to come, then please don't feel guilty. Maybe it is for the best. Good luck mate, and I hope I won't be seeing you soon.

The next day Jack was dead. My eyes were stinging and my heart felt so heavy that I could barely breathe. I picked up the whisky bottle and took a long pull at it. I waited for the firewater to kick-start my heart.

I read everything through again before switching off the computer and stowing the disk back where I had found it. Now I find the laboratory. But how? Perhaps it didn't exist anymore. Rutland had told Jack that the cargo had stopped coming on board soon after the fire, maybe the laboratory had closed down.

If it was at the Royal Air Force base and the laboratory had been connected with defence then it will be protected under the Official Secrets Act. That made some sense of all the killings. Special Branch would be keen to hush it up.

Could Simon's contacts at the Royal Society of Chemistry help? It was a thought and one which led me to think of Faye and Simon together. I took a risk and called Faye but she didn't answer. I left a message on her answer machine saying I would be away painting for a few days. My next call was to Simon but he wasn't answering either. I didn't leave a message. Neither did I call Jody, though I wanted to. Tomorrow I would tackle Brookfield.

'Adam!' Brookfield opened the door of his detached house. He glanced at his watch. I was damned if I was going to apologise for disturbing him at eight o'clock on a Saturday morning.

'A fire on board a ship on 4th July 1994, you filed the incident report,' I said tersely. I had hardly slept. I didn't have much time to get to the truth and I didn't like Brookfield.

Brookfield looked taken aback. 'Why do you want to know about that?'

'What was in that packing case, Des?'

'I can't remember every fire.'

'I think you'll remember this one. Who told you to say the incident report was missing?'

Brookfield looked genuinely puzzled. 'No one. They've been sent –'

'For computerisation.' I studied Brookfield's face and could see that he was telling the truth. Was I wrong? Was Brookfield innocent? *His mouth is full of ... deceit and fraud.*

'Why did you tell Ian to swap duty with Jack?'

'I didn't.'

'You were on the station that morning.'

'I didn't even speak to Ian or Jack. Look, what is all this?' Brookfield glanced nervously over his shoulder.

'Who did you tell their tallies had been switched over?'

'For Christ's sake, Adam, what are you talking about?'

'Who is it, Des?' A woman's voice called out.

'Just someone from the fire station,' Brookfield lied, stepping into the large front garden and closing the door to behind him.

I said, 'I'm talking about a fire on board a ship that has cost the lives of five fire fighters, not to mention two old men and possibly Ian. I think it's about time you told the truth about the *Mary Jane*.' At last I'd scored a direct hit. Brookfield's face paled.

He began walking away from the house towards the street where I had parked my bike.

He ran a hand through his thick dark hair and shifted nervously. 'I do remember the fire now but only because Mary Jane was my grandmother's name. I don't know what you mean about it causing deaths.'

'What happened at that fire?'

'I don't know. I wasn't there.'

'But you filed the report.'

'I did but I didn't go to it. I took a leave date. I didn't have any owing so I bought one off Colin Woodhall; I paid him to cover for me. I didn't want anyone to know I wasn't on duty.'

I could guess why. Brookfield had always had a reputation as a lady's man. He had been with a woman, conducting one of his affairs.

Brookfield said, 'Colin gave me the details and wrote the report and I signed it.'

I had been wrong. Brookfield wasn't involved. 'And he didn't hint there was anything unusual about the fire?'

'As far as he was concerned it was just a small and very straightforward fire.'

It seemed there was nothing more I could get from Brookfield.

'Aren't you going to tell me what's going on?' Brookfield called out, as I walked away.

'Forget I asked. And I'll forget you signed that incident report.'

I climbed on to my bike. Brookfield couldn't

lead me to that laboratory which meant I'd have to ask Simon. Who he didn't know involved in research wasn't worth knowing. I quickly risked checking my messages. There was nothing from Faye. I hadn't really expected anything and I wasn't going to phone home in case my phone was tapped.

I swung the bike out of the small cul de sac on to the road that led across the top of Portsdown Hill. Below me, to my left the city of Portsmouth and Hayling Island lay spread out in the grey morning light. My mobile rang. I had forgotten to switch it off. I pulled into the viewing spot and picnic area. There were two other cars parked but no occupants. Behind me the burger van was closed.

It was Jody.

'I've got some news for you,' she said, slightly breathlessly.

'Jody, I told you not to ask around.'

'I know but this is important. I know the name of the ship that was on fire. One of the pilots recalled it.'

'He's got a good memory,' I said, surprised.

'I mentioned to him about William Bransbury, the Minister, being at the port and that's how he recalled it. The ship was called the *Mary Jane*.'

'I know.'

'How?'

'Jack left me a message.'

'Where?'

'It doesn't matter. I need to find out what was on that ship.'

'Didn't Jack say?'

'No, only that he discovered it was chemicals from a laboratory somewhere on Salisbury Plain.'

'Christ! How did he discover that?'

'It's a long story.'

There was a pause before she said. 'What are you going to do now?'

'I'm going to find out who ran that laboratory.'

'How?'

'I'm going to ask my brother, Simon. He's a research scientist. If anyone can tell me it's Simon.'

'I want to help.'

'No,' I said firmly.

There was a pause before she said, 'You will call me, won't you?'

I promised I would. As I was about to pull out of the lay-by I glanced in my mirror and was surprised to see Motcombe, the gangly fire

fighter from Red Watch, emerge from one of the
footpaths and head towards a dark blue car. Still,
there was no reason why he shouldn't be here.
Perhaps he lived nearby and liked a walk in the
mornings. Perhaps he had a dog. I watched him
climb into the car. No dog followed. I hesitated
wondering whether or not to speak to him; did
he have any more information on Ian?

I was about to turn back when he answered
his mobile phone. I recalled that Red Watch were
on days. Motcombe must have a day off. I
decided that Ian couldn't help me now, so it was
pointless talking to Motcombe. I swung out of
the lay-by and headed for Bath.

CHAPTER 15

Harriet opened the door to me. She looked tired and she had been crying.

'Where's Simon?'

'He's at work.'

'I need the address, Harriet.'

'Of course,' she hesitated. 'Adam, can I talk to you for a moment.'

I wanted to refuse, time was ticking away, but the pleading in her eyes prevented me and I found myself following her down the hall and into a large and expensively equipped kitchen at the back of the house overlooking a splendid garden that led down to the canal.

'Simon's in trouble.'

My first thoughts were of Father. Had someone discovered Simon had pushed him down the stairs? But no, that was ridiculous. I had no proof of that. 'What kind of trouble?'

'He's… well… He's got himself into terrible debt. William's school called me this morning. They said that we haven't paid the fees for almost six months so I …' She took a deep breath. 'I broke into Simon's desk, and there are so many unpaid bills and his bank account is horrendously in arrears. There are threatening letters too and it seems his business is in trouble.'

'It should be out of it soon; he'll have Father's money.' I didn't mean to sound bitter but I couldn't help it.

'But that's just it, Adam. I know what he's done to you and why and I don't think it's right. I discovered some reports on you. Simon hired a private investigator to find you.'

'Why would he do that?' I asked surprised, but it did explain how he had got my telephone number.

'He wanted to make sure that you didn't

approach your father.' She looked decidedly ill at ease. She continued, 'Now I know now why he was in London every weekend. I thought he was having yet another affair and I've learnt to put up with them for the children's sake. It wasn't another woman this time, though. It was his father. Simon was bullying and cajoling him into making a will in his favour.'

And he wanted to make sure the field was clear of any possible interference from me.

Harriet went on, 'I've decided that I don't want any part of it, Adam. If you want to contest the will I'll tell them the truth. I've had enough of Simon's lies. But I can't leave him, I'd have nowhere to go and I have no money of my own.' She began to cry and I felt very sorry for her. 'I couldn't throw Simon out and he wouldn't go anyway. You know how forceful he can be.'

I did. Childhood memories rushed back of the times Simon had cajoled and bullied me into doing the things he wanted. 'I think I might have a way round that.'

'You might?'

I didn't like the hope in her voice, because it put too much pressure on me, but I had to do something to help her. I couldn't let Simon destroy her life as my father had tried to destroy mine.

She said, 'If you could get Simon to leave me then I could bring Daisy home. She's so unhappy.'

'Don't worry, I'll sort something out.' *If I live that long.* 'You'll have to trust me, Harriet.'

She nodded.

I gave her a smile of encouragement. 'Now where can I find Simon?'

She gave me the address and fifteen minutes later I was pulling up outside his offices and laboratory on a newly built and highly prestigious business park on the southern outskirts of the city. I parked in one of the visitors' slots next to Simon's Range Rover and gazed up at the modern three-storey glass fronted building. I wondered what had happened to the American deal, and if it was still going through.

The entrance door was locked so I rang the bell by the side of it. After a few seconds an attractive young woman in her mid thirties let me in and showed me into Simon's large office. It matched the rest of the building, wide smoked glass windows, chunky modern furniture, pastel-coloured walls and brightly coloured abstract art.

If this was anything to go by then I guessed there had been no expense spared over the laboratories either.

Simon looked at me cautiously. 'What do you want, Adam, I'm very busy.' He didn't bother to rise or invite me to sit. I didn't need to be invited. I crossed to the leather chair in front of Simon's desk and sat down.

'Nice place. The overheads must be huge.' I gazed around the room.

'I haven't got time for this.' Simon glared at me. I didn't comment. Instead I wondered how far he and Faye had gone?

Simon sighed. 'OK, let's get this over with.'

'I need a favour.' I saw Simon's surprise. Then his expression darkened.

'If it's about Father's will…'

I shook my head. 'It's not. You're welcome to the money, Simon. Your needs are greater than mine.'

Simon looked at me warily.

I went on, 'You must have a lot of bills to pay.' I waved my arm around the room. 'Father's money should help keep the creditors off your back and pay the school fees you owe.'

Simon slapped his hand down on the desk.

'You've been talking to Harriet. She's no bus –'

'She's every business, Simon,' I declared angrily. 'She's your wife, or perhaps you conveniently forget that? Anyway I don't give a fuck what you get up to and who you get up to it with, even if it is *my* wife.' Simon's eyes flickered with alarm. 'You can do what you like with your life and after this I shall go out of it for good. We don't have to see or speak to one another again, but before we part I want a favour. I reckon you owe me one, or maybe I will start to get more than curious as to why you visited Father so often in the last six months of his life and what you were doing in his study day after day and night after night when the sad bastard was suffering from dementia. I might even have enough to contest the will and with Harriet's help...'

'She wouldn't dare!' Simon cried, but I had him on the run. I could see that.

'I think you'll find she will. And if you don't see she's all right then I swear, Simon, that I will drag you through the courts until every single penny of our father's money has gone to the lawyers and your business is ruined. Now do you understand or do I –'

'You've made your point,' Simon snapped.

'What's this favour?'

'A laboratory somewhere on Salisbury Plain in July 1994 and for some time before it; I want to know who was running it and if possible what they were doing. It should be right up your street.'

I could see from his expression that it wasn't the favour he'd been expecting.

'And how am I supposed to find that out?'

'Use your extensive contacts. You're in the same business, so ask around.'

'What was the project?'

'I don't know but it involved experimenting with chemicals that cause cancer.'

'Christ, you're not asking much!'

'All I want is a name.'

'It's not possible.'

'It is, Simon,' I replied quietly and steadily. 'There can't be many laboratories on Salisbury Plain. I suggest you start by asking if anyone worked in or around the RAF base there.'

Simon looked at me as if I was barking mad. 'It'll be top secret then.'

'People still talk. Simon…'

'Ok. When do you want this information by?'

'Monday at the latest.'

He gave a hollow laugh. 'You've got to be joking. It could take me weeks.'

'I don't have weeks, Simon, and neither do you. I might not even have days.'

'What do you mean?' he asked sharply.

'People have already died because of it and if I'm not careful I might be next on the list. That should please you, Simon. And in case you're thinking of stalling me then I've made a written statement, which I will give it to Harriet,' I lied smoothly thinking that might not be a bad idea anyway.

'Have you gone mad?'

'You'd better start telephoning your contacts, Simon. I'll call you later.'

Simon hesitated.

'If I don't hear from you by Monday,' I continued, 'then I shall go to London and engage the most expensive lawyer I can find. I mean it.'

With an elaborate sigh and a raising of his eyebrows Simon picked up his phone. 'Jane, I don't want to take any calls for the rest of the day, unless they're from my brother, Adam. And I don't want to be disturbed. Just bring me a flask of coffee.'

I checked into a small family-run bed and

breakfast by the canal. I knew I was asking a lot of Simon but he was in the business of research and he did know a great many people in that field. I hoped he could get me the information by Monday but I didn't necessarily expect it. I checked my phone and saw that Steve had left me a message. I couldn't bring myself to ignore it. He might have some new information for me.

'Adam, at last! Where are you?'

'You told me to go away,' I said warily.

'Yes, but that was before…' he faltered.

My heart sank. I guessed there was a warrant out for my arrest.

Steve confirmed it with his next words. 'You're wanted for questioning in connection with the death of an old man called Rutland. We've got a file on you. It says you suffered a breakdown after a girl called Alison Lydeway died; she was Ben Harrow's sister. Why the hell didn't you tell me?'

'I didn't kill Ben and I didn't kill Rutland. He was already dead,' I replied crisply. 'How do you know about the file?'

'I'm back in Portsmouth. They needed extra officers for Rutland's murder.'

I didn't say anything but my mind was racing. Convenient that Steve should be called back, drafted into this investigation and then told about the file on me.

'What's going on, Adam?'

'You know what.'

I heard Steve draw in a breath. 'Come back and give yourself up.'

'Why? I haven't done anything.'

'We can give you protection.'

'We? Who are *we* Steve? The police? And protection from whom? Special Branch?' Steve's silence unnerved me. I couldn't believe Special Branch could be behind these killings, but I wondered if they knew who was. 'Did they ask you to call me? Are they tracing this call?'

'Turn yourself in, Adam. Let's get this business cleared up.'

I switched off my mobile and checked out of the bed and breakfast. I wasn't sure where I could go that was safe – perhaps nowhere. Steve had been told to call me. Special Branch knew I had come here to speak to Simon and they'd ask him why? Would Simon tell them? Probably, if it meant getting me off his back. How long would it take them to get to Simon? Would it be before he could give me some idea of who might have been conducting that research?

I drove across the bridge into Wales and found myself a small hotel in Cardiff where I spent another sleepless night. The next morning I telephoned Simon from a call box. No joy, but neither did I get any indication that the police or Special Branch had been to see him.

I walked by the harbour my mind turning to Faye. I wondered how many times she had been unfaithful. How many times had she slept with someone in that flat in Convent Garden? I examined my feelings for her and found them devoid of love. I felt only sadness that it hadn't worked out but even that was tinged with relief. If I came through this I would leave her. I didn't think she'd be heart broken.

On Monday I rang Simon from a payphone across the road.

'At last. I've been waiting for you to call. Why did you switch your mobile off?'

'You've got a name? I asked surprised. That was much quicker than I dared hope.

'Gerry Drake.'

'Where can I find him?'

'In a cemetery in Devizes.'

'He's dead?'

'I don't think he decided to quit science to

become a gravedigger. Of course he's dead. He was killed in a fire.'

Another bloody fire! Had that been started deliberately like Jack's and Honeyman's or was it accidental and a mere coincidence? 'What kind of fire?'

'How the hell should I know,' Simon screamed with exasperation. 'A house fire, I suppose. Does it matter?'

Oh yes, it matters. Aloud I asked, 'When?'

'What the hell is all this about?'

'When?'

There was a short pause on the other end then, '1995.'

I knew it. 'Do you know if he was working with anyone?'

'No. You wanted a name and I've given it to you. It's the best I can do.'

I rang off, pausing for a moment to gather my thoughts: perhaps he had given me any old name to get me off his back. I headed for Devizes.

It didn't take me long to reach the small Wiltshire market town. I asked an elderly man for directions to the cemetery and found it not far from the canal. My heart sank at the size of it.

The records office was closed so there was nothing for it but to cover the ground methodically until I found the grave that I was looking for.

It was a bleak grey day and the naked trees afforded no protection from a sharp wind. The graves looked forlorn and abandoned as I trudged among them. Eventually I found what I was looking for on the far side, bordering undulating fields. I stared down at the black marble headstone. It was simple enough. *Gerald Drake 5.5. 1950 - 3.4.1995, 'Beloved son and father.'* Not husband? Was he widowed, divorced? There were flowers on the grave, real ones not plastic, and they were fresh. Who still mourned Gerald Drake? His mother or father? Or perhaps a son or daughter? Someone at least who might be able to tell me something of Drake's work and the circumstances of his death.

I wrote down the dates and returned to the bike. Ten minutes later I was in the small sub office of the *Wiltshire Gazette*, just off the market square, where I was told if I needed to access the archives I would have to go to Swindon where 'head office' was.

As the time ticked by I set out for Swindon

and decided that a call at the library might be more helpful than the newspaper office. With some difficulty and many frustrations I finally managed to locate it and persuade the librarian to allow me access to the microfiche and the local newspaper archives.

As I settled down to scan through the obituaries and reports of 1995 my stomach rumbled and I realised it was mid afternoon. But I didn't have time to eat. I had to find someone who knew, or was related, to Gerald Drake, and who knew what had happened in 1994.

I began by looking through the notices of death; this time at least I had a date. There were several notices for the few days after Drake's death, from relatives, friends and colleagues and religiously I wrote the names down though few gave their surnames. Still I could see that there was a 'beloved daughter,' who might be able to tell me something. There was nothing that referred to Drake as 'son', neither was there anything for 'husband'. There were a couple of 'nephews'. What I didn't have was addresses, but the telephone directory might be able to furnish some at least and failing that the undertakers. I noted where flowers could be sent, a journey that would take me back to Devizes.

Frowning with impatience and worried that time was running out, I spun back the microfiche to see if there were any reports on the fire that had killed Gerald Drake. In my haste I almost missed it. There was a picture of what looked to have once been a large, country house, gutted by fire, and in the foreground were a couple of firemen and a fire appliance. The headline ran, *'House fire claims scientist's life.'*

In anticipation I read the article.

A fire has claimed the life of eminent scientist Dr Gerald Drake (45). Four fire appliances were called to a fire at Dr Drake's house in the early hours of Monday morning after reports of smoke and flames were seen by Dr Drake's nearest neighbour half a mile away. After a search by fire fighters wearing breathing apparatus, Doctor Drake's body was discovered in the drawing room. The six-bedroom former manor house, thought to date back to the 1700s, has been almost completely destroyed. There was no one else in the house at the time of the fire although it was believed that his daughter had arrived home from university for the weekend.

Dr Drake was an eminent biochemist and a member of the Royal Society of Chemistry. He had published many scientific papers and was a renowned specialist of genetic research. Police have not ruled out the possibility of arson and animal liberationists, as Dr Drake had been the target of these in the past when his groundbreaking research identified brain-clogging proteins that cause dementia.

Dr Drake, who is divorced, leaves a daughter Joanne (22).

So Simon would have known Drake quite well. Their paths must have crossed both being experts in genetics. It was typical of Simon not to tell me more and silently I cursed my brother.

I quickly scrolled onwards until I found coverage of the funeral. The photographer had taken a shot of the grieving crowd dressed in black on what looked like a bright and blustery April day. I stared hard at the photograph. Standing stiffly in the middle of the group was a slender young woman in her early twenties. She was dressed in black trousers and a black jacket. A hat was pulled down low over her forehead, her eyes were mournful, her expression bereft.

The newspaper report named her as Joanne Drake. I knew her by a different name: Jody Piers.

I felt a stab at my heart. Why had she lied to me?

With churning emotions I left the library. I needed some air. I needed to time to think through the implications of this. I needed space.

Before I realised it I was through Devizes. The day was drawing in. Visibility was poor as I drove through the bleak rainswept countryside. I had only half my mind on the road the other half was trying to come to grips with what I had just learned.

Why hadn't she told me about her father? Why let me stumble on blindly? Did she hope that I would give up and when she saw that I wasn't going to she had given me the name of the ship? A name that she had known all the time. How had she conveniently found lodgings next door to Jack? Had she really been in London on the day of Jack's funeral or had she ransacked Jack's house in search of his disks and diary? Why?

Perhaps she didn't know what her father had been doing in that research laboratory and wanted to find out? Or perhaps she *did* know and she was desperate to keep secret the fact that he had been exporting something that had caused cancer. How had she known that Jack was investigating it though? Had Jack confided in her? Is that what he meant when he said his mouth was full of deceit and fraud, except that he meant *her* mouth?

I recalled my first meeting with Jody – her head sticking out of the window to greet me. I remembered how she had happened to be jogging along the promenade on the day I had discovered Jack's message. Then she had been in the dockyard after I had spoken to Sandy Ditton and finally that telephone call before I headed for Bath. God what a fool I'd been! My feelings for her had blinded me. She had deliberately set out to get close to me in order to discover how much I knew and I had told her I was going to Simon. A chill ran down my spine. How far would she go to stop me?

What had Gerald Drake been doing? Could it conceivably have something to do with chemical warfare? Perhaps it concerned the trial of a new drug or substance that had been exported illegally overseas and sold to terrorists for which Drake would have been handsomely paid. Was Jody's father a traitor? Is that why she was so desperate that no one should get to the truth?

Behind the pain of my hurt was a smouldering anger. I didn't like being used.

I dropped a gear and increased my speed. I rode past RAF Upavon and on to the Salisbury Plain. Out of nowhere a car came racing up behind me. He must have been doing a ton. He had his full beam on, blinding me. I waved my arm to try and tell him to lower his lights but it didn't work. I slowed down hoping the idiot would overtake me. He didn't. He stayed behind. I felt the first flutter of fear. He flashed his lights at me. Perhaps it was the police. They had traced me.

The lights flashed again and again. He was flagging me down but I couldn't see any indication that it was an unmarked police car and I wasn't going to stop to find out. I could out ride him. The bike had greater speed and manoeuvrability than a car. But just as I made up my mind to do it a lorry emerged from one of the dips in the road and was heading full pelt towards me, lights blazing, horn blaring as the car behind me pulled out to overtake me. I had no option but to apply the brakes as the driver behind me seemed intent on killing himself. With the blood rushing through my ears and my heart in overdrive the bike went into a skid, the car shot past me with inches to spare, the lorry roared away. I sped off the road over the soft wet earth, felt myself catapulted into the air and hit the ground.

CHAPTER 16

It was pitch black when I awoke. It was also raining heavily. My head hurt so much I thought it might burst and every part of my body ached. With an effort and much grunting and groaning I heaved myself up. I pulled off my helmet and felt the rain lashing my face. I had to get into the dry and warm, but I was in the middle of nowhere.

I staggered up. I felt dizzy and sank to my knees. I took a deep breath and tried again a few seconds later. This time I succeeded. I was getting fed up with being a target. I was going to make as much bloody trouble as I could before the bastards tried again.

I peered into the dark night, wondering in which direction was the road. I didn't want to risk stumbling off deeper on to the plains. If I did, I'd probably die of hypothermia. There was nothing for it but to wait until I saw a passing car's headlights. It was difficult with the wind beating against me and my head pounding, but I scoured the black night until, some minutes later, I had sight of a car and got my bearings. I set off in the direction of the road and was surprised and relieved to find it less than a half a mile away. Now all I had to do was wait for a car, or lorry, that would let me hitch a lift. Looking the way I must, I didn't hold out a great deal of hope. Several cars passed me before a lorry ground to a halt and wincing with pain I stumbled towards it. I climbed into the cab with a heartfelt sigh of relief and much gratitude.

The driver said he was heading for the ferry port at Portsmouth. Fate it seemed was taking me back there, and once there I knew what I had to do no matter what the consequences. I had to confront Jody.

I caught a taxi to the marina where I showered and changed into dry clothes. Then I called her.

'Adam, at last! Where have you been? I've been worried about you.'

I bet. Worried that whoever she was working with hadn't succeeded in killing me. Or had Jody been driving that car? 'Can you meet me?' I wondered if she would notice a new hardness in my voice.

She didn't seem to. 'Of course, where?'

'Northney Marina, Hayling Island. I'll meet you outside the marina office in about twenty minutes.'

I hovered at the marina entrance until her small car pulled in. There was no one behind her or in front of her.

'Let's walk.' I took her arm and we set off towards the boatyard. It had stopped raining. She said nothing. 'I expect you're surprised to see me,' I said after a moment. I couldn't keep the bitterness out of my voice.

'What's happened, Adam? Clearly something has.'

I spun round to stare at her. 'As if you don't know. It didn't work Jody. I'm still alive.'

'What are you talking about? Has someone

tried to kill you?' She looked aghast.

I laughed scornfully. 'Was it you driving that car?'

'Adam, please you're not making any sense.'

'Good try, Jody, but it's over. I know who you are. How well do you know my brother? Did he call you to say that he had given me your father's name?' She was staring at me bemused. I continued. 'Did you kill Jack or did you have help? Are you shagging Brookfield as well as my brother? Did you get Brookfield to tell you about the tallies being switched? Did you tell him I was going to look out the fire reports so he'd better say they had gone for computerisation?'

In the dim lights along the edge of the marina I could see her astounded expression. She was almost as good an actress as Faye.

'I know about your father,' I said abruptly. I saw her stiffen. I wanted to shake the truth from her. It took a great deal of effort to control myself. This was a woman who had made me love her. I wanted to hurt her. 'Was he betraying his country is that why you can't let the truth come out?'

A flicker of pain crossed her face before her expression changed to anger. I experienced a moment of doubt.

'My father was not a traitor,' she blazed. 'And neither am I a killer or a slut. I don't know your brother and I have never met Brookfield.'

Was I wrong? How could I be? It all fitted together. No, she wasn't going to deceive me again. The anger bubbled up in me and burst forth. 'How many more people are going to die because of your lies?'

'I didn't mean –'

'Did you have anything to do with Jack's death?' I grabbed her roughly by the arms.

'You can't think –'

'Did you?' I shouted.

'No,' she shouted back. 'You want to know why your friend was killed in that fire and I need to know why my father suffered the same fate. It's taken me five years to get this far and I still don't know the name of the bastard who killed him. I thought Jack, and then you, might find out who he is.'

I stared at her a moment longer. She held my gaze. Finally I released her. It didn't mean I believed her.

'What was your father researching?' I snapped.

'I don't know. I've been trying to find out. I've talked to everyone who knew him, who worked with him. I've spoken to my father's friends, all my relatives. All I discovered was that he worked on various projects part funded by the Department of Health and part funded by a medical research charity. The charity was based in Portsmouth. I came here. I met Jack.'

'How?' I still didn't trust her.

'Purely by coincidence. No, it was. When I found out my father had worked in Portsmouth I applied to undertake a research project in the harbour. I met Jack when he came to the dockyard on an exercise and we got talking. I was staying in a small hotel but needed to find something cheaper. He said his next door neighbour was looking for a lodger.'

I didn't believe her. 'When was this?'

'Early October.' She looked away. I knew she was lying. She continued, 'Someone was working with my father. He's the man who killed my father and Jack. He's the man who can tell us what was really going on in that laboratory and I intend to find him.'

I turned and began walking back towards the marina. She followed. There were still so many questions that she hadn't answered. I could press her yet I knew her answers would be more lies.

'Adam, what are you going to do now?'

I wasn't about to tell her. I drew up. Inside the marina office were two men; they were talking to the duty manager and they didn't look like sailors. I had to think quickly. I grabbed Jody's arm and pulled her back out of sight. 'You were followed.'

'I didn't see anyone.'

I swung her round so that she was facing me. 'Do you want me to find out who was working with your father?' I said urgently.

'Yes.'

'Then do as I say. Go back to your car and drive it round to the hotel. Stop there with the engine running and get out.'

'But what –'

'No questions,' I barked.

She considered for a brief moment. Then, 'OK.'

I watched her head towards the car park. Would she do as I asked? The two men inside the marina office didn't turn round. She started the engine. I ran through the boatyard until I came out by the entrance to the marina with the hotel opposite me. She climbed out, a puzzled expression on her face. I jumped in.

'I'll be in touch.'

I sped away. In my rear view mirror I saw her looking after me. No one followed me.

Just beyond Petersfield I pulled into a service station and sat for a few minutes before heading inside for something to eat. I stared into my coffee and ate my bacon sandwich. Blotting out the tinny Christmas songs that pervaded the steamy warmth of the café I tried to put the pieces of the jigsaw together. I didn't believe that cock and bull story she'd given me about just bumping into Jack. I didn't believe anything she had said except that her father was Drake and I knew that for a fact. What was she doing now? Had she called her accomplice and told him I was driving her car? She didn't know where I was heading though.

And the two men in the marina? I guessed they were Special Branch. Perhaps they had been following Jody? Would they question her? Maybe they had already done so. Had she called them when I had telephoned and asked her to meet me? That made some kind of sense if she didn't want me to discover the truth about her father; if she couldn't kill me then she could have me arrested. Sure, I could spout something about

Drake and his research project, but Special Branch would ensure that either I wasn't believed, or that I would never be allowed to speak out about it. Special Branch didn't need to silence Jody because they knew that she would never want her father's treachery to be made public. And the person who had worked with Drake – was there one? Or was that pure fabrication too?

I finished my coffee and the last of my sandwich without tasting it, and called Simon from the public telephone in the corridor between the ladies' and gents' toilets. Harriet answered.

'He's not here, Adam. He said he had to go to London to sort out your father's affairs.'

I could hear the wariness in her voice. 'Then he's staying at the house?'

'Probably.' Then she added, 'He might not be alone.'

Faye? Was Simon with her? I rang off after telling her that I'd be in touch later.

The service station car park wasn't very full. I crossed to Jody's car but before I had gone half way a car pulled in behind it. I slowed my steps. In the car were the two men I'd seen in the marina office. How had they followed me here? Jody didn't know where I was heading. But then perhaps they didn't need to tail me. Perhaps Jody's car had some kind of tracking device in it. Was she aware of that I wondered?

I tapped my pockets as if I'd forgotten something then swiftly did an about turn and headed back to the service station. I called into the café area and my table as though to collect what I'd forgotten and glanced out of the window at the car. One of the men was missing from it.

I quickly left the café but instead of turning out of the exit I headed for the gents' toilet. Before reaching it I did a swift turn to the left with a quick glance over my shoulder; no one was behind me. I ran outside and as luck would have it a lorry driver was just climbing into his vehicle.

'Could you give me a lift, mate?' I called out.

The man poised, one foot on the step up into his cab. 'Where do you want to go?'

'London.'

'Then you're in luck. Hop in.'

He dropped me outside the Embankment and I caught the circle line to Victoria, from where I walked to Father's house. I pressed my finger on the bell and kept it there until a light went on in the hall.

'What the fuck do you think you're playing at?' Simon raged throwing open the door.

'I rather think that's my line.' I stepped over the threshold, surprising my brother with my assertiveness. 'You can tell Faye to come down, or shall I go up.' I paused with my foot on the bottom stair.

Simon looked as though he had dressed hastily, since his shirt was hanging out. He wore no tie, socks or shoes. He seemed to be on the point of denying that Faye was there, then shrugged and headed towards the kitchen calling as he went, 'Faye, it's your husband.'

As if she doesn't already know! Simon must have peered out of the window and seen me. I stayed where I was, my body rigid with tension, wondering what emotions would course through me when I saw her. Within a few seconds she appeared at the top of the stairs and glowered at me. I couldn't help smiling to myself. With Faye I would always be in the wrong.

'What on earth are you doing here?' she declared angrily.

I was amazed at her cheek. 'Aren't I suppose to say that?'

She raised her beautifully plucked eyebrows. She'd even had time to renew her lipstick. 'I don't know what you mean. I'm here helping Simon sort through your father's things.'

Oh, that was good. It was almost believable. The old me would have probably apologised. Now I saw the steely glint in her eyes that betrayed selfishness, the tightness of her mouth and the tilt of her chin that should have warned me years ago that Faye always got what she wanted.

'It won't work, Faye, not this time. I'm not interested in who you've been screwing, including my brother.'

She stared at me for a moment, as she calculated which way to jump: a straight denial or something serpentine? Seeing my expression, she must have decided the time for more fairy tales was over. As she descended the stairs, I thought I saw relief on her face. She pushed past me and I followed her to the kitchen where Simon was sitting at the table with a whisky bottle and glass in front of him. He glanced at us and took a swig of his drink.

It was Faye who spoke first. 'I don't think you've got any cause to be so bloody righteous, Adam. You do realise the police have been to see me at work. You've put my whole career in jeopardy.'

'I doubt it.'

'You're wanted for murder, for heaven's sake!'

She reached across Simon and poured herself a glass of whisky. Neither of them offered me one. Simon glanced up at me a wary expression on his face, which, now that I looked closer, I could see was etched with worry. To him Faye had just been available and willing. I guessed that Simon's need for sex was a compulsion and already he was beginning to regret being involved with her.

'Simon's told me about Alison.' Faye shuddered beautifully, but instead of making me angry or defensive it made me laugh. That stung her to retort, 'I don't think it's anything to smile about. God, if only I'd known all these years that I'd been living with a madman and a probable murderer.'

'Lucky I don't want to kill *you*, then.' I marvelled at my ability to be so flippant about something that would certainly have sent me over the edge a few weeks earlier. Simon's head came up; he had obviously noticed the change in me.

'Don't worry, Faye. You can have your divorce,' I said. 'If Harriet leaves Simon, perhaps the two of you can team up. I think you suit one another admirably.'

'What do you want, Adam?' Simon interrupted sharply.

'I want her to leave.'

'You'd better go, Faye,' Simon said, glancing at her. Faye looked furious.

'I will not.'

'For Christ's sake, get out.' Simon shouted.

Faye flushed. Her eyes flicked between us, and clearly aware that she was not going to be the focus of attention, replied vindictively, 'Sod you then. Sod you both. You'll be hearing from my lawyers, Adam.' She flounced from the room. 'You can collect your things from the house, including your sodding cat and don't bother coming to my parents for Christmas.'

If I hadn't been so worried I might have cheered.

Neither Simon nor I spoke until we heard the front door bang shut a few minutes later. Then I said, 'OK, I want to know who was working with Drake?'

'What is all this about Drake?' Simon said wearily. 'What is going on, Adam? The police haven't been to question me yet but no doubt they will. I can't afford to have a brother of mine splashed across the Sunday newspapers, wanted for murder. I've already lost the American finance deal but I've got the chance of going in with someone else. You're not going to ruin that for me.'

'Just tell me who Drake was working with, Simon,' I said.

'I don't know.'

I made to leave. 'Have it your own way, but if I get caught by the police I'm going to tell them that I don't think Father fell down the stairs. You pushed him.'

Simon paled. 'They won't believe you.' He tried to bluff it out but I could see he was nervous.

'No? Who had a private detective follow me to make sure I stayed away? Who inherits everything? Who spent hours with him before he died? Who is in debt?'

Simon sprang out of his chair and paced the

room. The terrible truth of how far my brother might have gone to get hold of the money sucked the breath from me.

Simon said, 'He was old. He was ill and confused. He fell.'

'Convenient, though, for you. Were you really in meetings in Bath that morning? Perhaps I should check. Just think what the newspapers would do with that. Then there's Faye; my brother screwing my wife. The tabloids will love it.'

I heard Simon's laboured breathing above the ticking of the grandfather clock in the hall. I couldn't see his expression because his back was to me.

'Who gave you Drake's name?' I said quietly.

Simon spun round. 'Does it matter? You asked me to find out. I did.'

'But who told you?' I persisted.

'You've gone mad. Why this obsession?' But it was bluster.

'Simon…'

He returned to the table to pour himself another whisky. Finally he said, 'Tim Davenham.'

It was my turn to look surprised. I recalled Davenham at my father's funeral: the tall, good-looking man. My brain began to slot the pieces into place. Davenham must have taken my file from the back of my motorbike. Why? Because he must have been working on the project with Drake. He had given Drake's name to Simon and set me up so that he could be ahead of me when I went to Devizes, and then he had tried to kill me on Salisbury Plain. Jody and Davenham wanted to ensure that the secret research project remained just that: secret. My fist clenched and a chill entered my heart.

Steeling myself for his answer, I said, 'What made you ask Davenham?'

'It was fortuitous really. He called me on Sunday. He wants to put some money into one of my research projects; we had discussed it at Father's funeral. I told him you wanted to find out about this laboratory on Salisbury Plain.'

Oh yes, how fortuitous. If I wanted proof that Jody was working with Davenham then there it was. It didn't explain the men in the marina though, or the fact that her car was fitted with a tracking device, unless Special Branch were keeping an eye on her as well as me. I still didn't have all the answers but I would soon.

'Davenham's address, Simon?' I demanded.

Simon nursed his whisky.

'I need it now,' I said firmly.

He stared at me a moment longer, then with a shrug gave it to me.

Chapter 17

By the time I reached Davenham's home in Mayfair it had stopped raining but the wind was gathering in strength.

I wasn't stupid enough to think that after confronting Davenham he'd let me quietly go back to Portsmouth and resume my career as a marine artist. This was the end of the line. Soon I would know it all. And soon, said the small voice inside my head, you'll be dead like Jack.

I rang the bell and waited with my heart knocking against my ribs, from anticipation not fear. There were none of the symptoms of the panic attacks that had once tormented me. My fury was making me bold, and perhaps even foolish, but I didn't care.

The door drew open and Davenham was smiling at me. 'Adam, come in, I've been expecting you.' His voice was silky smooth.

I wanted to round on him there and then, to hit that smug, smiling countenance, but I forced myself to wait. Time for that later, when I had the answers, I told myself, as he showed me into a large, splendidly proportioned room, elegantly and extravagantly furnished.

Davenham said, 'You're very persistent, I must say. It would have been better for you if you hadn't been.'

I should have been afraid but I wasn't. This was the end, the truth. And even if he didn't kill me, or I managed to escape, I was still glad I had come. I vowed that before I went I would do something to hurt him, to take revenge.

I said, 'You were responsible for giving those fire fighters cancer and for killing Jack.'

'I haven't killed anyone.'

I tensed myself in anger; I wanted to ram my fist into his grinning face.

'Why don't you take off your wet jacket,' he suggested politely. 'I don't think you'll be needing it again, and you're dripping water all over the parquet flooring.'

I ignored him. He shrugged as if to say please yourself and waved me into a seat easing himself in the seat opposite, pinching up his beautifully tailored light grey trousers, and crossing his legs.

I didn't sit but continued to loom over him. I could take him at any time. I was strong, fit and younger than him. Was he alone in the house, though? If I attacked him here and now would someone come running? Would they call the police? What chance did I have then of setting the record straight? No one would believe the word of a man wanted for murder against an affluent and respected man like Davenham. I listened for any sound that might tell me if the house was occupied, but apart from the ticking of a clock there was nothing.

Davenham went on, 'If it's murder you're talking about, I rather think it's you the police want.'

'You took my file from my bike, when I went back inside to say goodbye to Faye.'

'Of course.'

'And you tried to force me off the road in a Mercedes.'

'I don't normally do that sort of thing but I thought it might be fun. I didn't expect you to be riding home so slowly.'

'How did you know where to find me?' Then I answered my own question. 'Simon told you of course but you couldn't have got ahead of me on the dual carriageway,' I added, puzzled as I tried to work out the timing of the incident.

'No, that wasn't Simon. You were being followed anyway, not only by that boy, Ben Lydeway, but by Special Branch.'

I already knew that. 'Because of Jack?'

'He just wouldn't give it up.'

'How do *you* know Special Branch were following me?'

'Because of me.' A tall, gangly man stepped out from the dining room.

I was astounded to see it was Pete Motcombe from Red Watch. It took a fraction of a second for my mind to connect him with Jack's last message to me. *His mouth is full of deceit and fraud.* My mind raced, rewinding conversations I'd had with Motcombe trying to find any sign or clue of his deception. Hatred and anger course through me. I clenched my fists and glared at him.

'You arranged for Jack to swap duties with Ian to make sure he would go into that fire first,' I said. Then the blood froze in my veins. Ian? He was missing. 'You bastard.' I spat. I was beyond fear. Anger consumed me. I lunged out and grabbed Motcombe by the throat before a violent blow struck me on the side of my head. I fell to the floor.

Someone kicked me in the stomach. I doubled up with pain. I heard snatches of conversation before I was hauled up and thrust in a chair.

'Let's have no more heroics, Adam,' Davenham said sternly.

With a throbbing head and a sore stomach I wasn't in very good physical shape to attempt them, but the fury inside me was far from subdued. It had been stupid of me to attack Motcombe. If I wanted to get out of this alive then I'd have to do better than that. I had to use my brain. I needed time to think. I also had to know the truth.

'How did you get on the watch, Motcombe?'

'I was transferred from London, or so my cover story went. Everyone accepted me for who I was, including you.'

'But I still don't understand, if you're with Special Branch then what are you doing helping this murdering bastard?'

Davenham laughed.

Motcombe said, 'Let's say that Special Branch have a special interest in Mr Davenham, and so do I.'

It clicked at last. 'You're working for Special Branch and for him.' I jerked my head in Davenham's direction and then wished I hadn't as a sharp pain shot through it.

'I told you he was clever,' Motcombe tossed at Davenham.

I wished I was clever enough to find a way out of this. I said, 'Special Branch put you into Red Watch when Jack started getting curious about those deaths and the fire. How did you know what he was doing? Who told you?' Jody, of course. My heart sank at the extent of her deception.

Motcombe said, 'I don't think you need to know that.'

Davenham disagreed. 'It won't do any harm to tell him, after all he's not going to be around long enough to repeat it.'

'Suit yourself.'

Davenham rose to fetch himself a drink. My eyes flicked to Motcombe wondering if I could take him. Motcombe read my thoughts. 'Don't even think it, Adam. I am trained to kill.'

'Drink, Adam?'

'Why not.'

'I think you'd be more comfortable if you removed your sailing jacket.'

After a moment's delay, I stood up and did so wondering if I threw it at one of them, would it cause enough of a distraction for me to make my escape? But Motcombe's protruding eyes never left me. As Davenham handed me the drink Motcombe took a gun from his pocket.

I wouldn't be able to overpower the two of them and escape a possible gunshot wound. Motcombe was a professional he wouldn't miss. The odds were stacked too high.

'So come on, who told you what Jack was doing?' I wanted to hear Davenham tell me it was Jody. I had to know for certain.

'Bransbury, the Minister for the Environment, Energy and Waste.'

I started. It wasn't the answer I had been expecting. When I recovered from my surprise my heart sank. Now I understood.

Motcombe took up the explanation. 'Bransbury's telephone was tapped. He had double-crossed one political party, he might do it again. He was vulnerable to blackmail having crossed the floor. And he is gay.'

Davenham must have seen my surprise because he said:

'No one knows. Not even his wife.'

There was something in Davenham's tone of voice that made me wonder. Was Davenham his lover?

'Rutland telephoned me after your friend Jack visited Honeyman,' Davenham explained. 'Honeyman had called the gallant captain to say that Jack Bartholomew was asking questions about a certain cargo that was carried in 1994. I had to warn Bill. The Minister for the Environment, Energy and Waste involved in disposing of hazardous waste and possibly causing the death of those firemen? Can you imagine the scandal?'

'So this is where you came in, Motcombe. You had to hush things up?'

'I was sent in to find out what the secret was that could cause a scandal and possibly wreck the government. Jack was good, he led me to

Honeyman and Honeyman led me to Rutland. After a little pressure Rutland told me who had paid him to take the cargo.'

'And you thought you'd earn yourself some extra money?'

Davenham said, 'I'm a wealthy man, Greene, and everyone has their price, even your brother.'

My mind was racing. How could I go for Motcombe and get that gun from him? How long did I have?

'What was in that cargo?' I asked tersely. 'You can at least tell me that before you kill me.' For a moment I thought of Simon but Davenham must have read my mind.

'I shouldn't rely on Simon coming to your rescue. As I said, everyone has his price. He'll soon get through your father's inheritance, my offer of help will be rescinded, and that will be the end of him unless he plays ball. Simon, as you must know, doesn't care about anyone or anything except success and that means continuing his research and getting his product to market.'

I felt some pity for Simon. 'The cargo?' I prompted. There just had to be a way out of this. 'It came from the laboratory on Salisbury Plain?'

Davenham answered. 'Yes. I was researching into developing a new anti-ageing drug. The project was highly secret as you can imagine; if competitors got a sniff of what I was doing there would have been no end to the industrial espionage. It was a government project; Bill helped me get the funding for it. At the time he was a Conservative MP. I convinced him of the need to look into researching a drug that could help keep people fitter and healthier longer. I was working with an enzyme called telomerase. It was first discovered in 1984. Telomerase is found in a wide variety of cancers which have a genetic mutation allowing them to manufacture telomerase.'

'You've lost me,' I muttered.

Davenham smiled patronizingly. 'In the 1970s it was discovered that the ends of our chromosomes have little, er shall we say, caps on them which prevent them from getting frayed. If these caps, called telomeres, are lost, then the chromosomes stick together and the cell eventually dies. More cells die, the more you age. In a normal cell the telomeres fuse gradually becomes shorter and shorter and eventually the cell commits suicide. We grow old.'

'So by using this enzyme and manufacturing telomerase you can stop the cell committing suicide and prevent, or hold up, the ageing process?'

'In its simplistic way, yes. We're all living longer – well some of us are.' He grinned.

My body stiffened. The adrenaline was pumping through me preparing me to attack. I thought what have I got to lose? But not yet. Motcombe wouldn't kill me here; it was too risky. They would have to take me somewhere, and maybe only Motcombe would do that. One against one, even with a gun I stood a better chance of staying alive.

Davenham was saying, 'If we could just slow down the ageing process and therefore stave off some of the diseases of old age, Parkinson's, cancer, osteoarthritis… Oh I know they're not confined to the elderly but the majority of cases, except possibly cancer, are. Just think of the savings to the NHS. The elderly and their ailments are a great drain on it.'

'So it was done purely for the good of the country to help save the National Health Service money,' I scoffed, tossing back some of the whisky, which until then had stayed untouched in my hands.

Davenham shrugged. 'It would have had commercial implications too, of course, but I didn't worry too much about that then. I just wanted my own laboratory and to conduct my research. I had ideas, which I wanted to test. I had met Bill at university, which is where I also met your brother, as you know. I lost touch with Bill for a few years before coming across him again at a dinner. I told him about my ideas and he agreed to help.'

I bet he did, after Davenham had seduced him and then blackmailed him. I also presumed the relationship was still active.

Davenham swirled the whisky in the beautifully cut crystal glass with his slim elegant hands. 'During the course of my research I experimented with many chemicals, which included what are coarsely known as gender benders – PBDEs – polybrominated diphenyl ethers – if you want the full name. They disrupt hormones, and are known endocrine disrupters, which damage sperm. The processes also involved the use of Acrylamide, a suspected carcinogen, but there isn't sufficient data to prove it causes cancer in humans. After all, how can you test it on humans to see if it is known to cause cancer?'

He rose and poured another whisky. I eyed Motcombe, wondering if I would have a chance to escape that gun but Motcombe's gaze was clearly on me and the gun was steady.

Davenham continued, 'The process of disposing of carcinogens requires precautions, which even from the brief time you spent studying biochemistry you should know, but in case your breakdown has obliterated the knowledge I'll tell you. For example they must be doubly wrapped in plastic bags, sealed and labelled, clearly identified and passed on to a specialist waste disposal company.'

'And you didn't bother with any of that!' I spat.

Davenham shrugged. 'I had an arrangement with a certain party overseas who would take the waste for a fee and dispose of it. There was nothing illegal in that, at least there wasn't then.'

'For Christ's sake, men have died because of you!'

'I didn't start the fire.'

I was out of my chair but Motcombe was quicker. He struck me across the face with the butt of the gun. I put a hand up to my bleeding mouth.

Davenham shook his head. 'Give him a handkerchief, Motcombe; I don't want his blood all over the furniture. Really, Adam, you shouldn't be so emotional. Frank Rutland knew what he was carrying. He made money out of me though you wouldn't have thought so to look at the way he was living.'

'Did you kill him?' I asked surprised.

'Of course not, and neither did I kill Honeyman. That needed more expertise.'

I glanced at Motcombe who simply shrugged. I knew it was him.

Davenham went on, 'After the fire on board the ship, Rutland got a little nervous but there was no evidence to show that it had caused cancer. We carried on until 1995 when the Basel Convention examined the exporting of waste. What we had been doing until then, exporting waste to be disposed of in another country, wasn't illegal.'

'But not marking it as hazardous waste, was,' I snapped. 'Those fire fighters went on to that ship not knowing that they were being exposed to dangerous chemicals. Why not get the waste from your laboratory experiments disposed of in the proper manner? Surely the laboratory was perfectly legitimate? This can't be just about money,' I cried incredulously.

'Isn't everything about money at the end of the day?' answered Davenham. 'Besides I didn't trust anyone. A chemist at a waste disposal company could have easily tracked me down and discovered what I was doing. I couldn't afford anyone to find out. That's why it was only me, oh and Gerry Drake. Unfortunately he died.'

I thought of Jody. Had her father known what Davenham was doing with that waste, or had he been innocent of the blatant negligence that Davenham had practised?

Davenham said, 'The research led to no anti-ageing drug, but I'm still working on it, although I did find that what I had produced had remarkable results for rejuvenating skin, hence the April range of beauty products and rejuvenating skin creams. It's made me a very wealthy man, as you can see.'

I looked at Motcombe. 'You made sure that gas cylinder was placed inside the club and ready to explode when Jack went in. Did you push Jack into the fire or simply let him go before you.'

'Jack was always an action man.' He smiled.

I jumped up and flung the remaining dregs of my drink in Motcombe's face. But Motcombe's response was quicker. The gun came down on the side of my head. I didn't stand a chance. My world went dark.

CHAPTER 18

When I awoke I was lying on my side and something hard was rubbing against my cheek. I shifted my head and winced, cursing softly under my breath as gravel pierced my skin. I tried to move my hands but found they were tied behind my back. It was dark. It took me four attempts and a great deal of effort to swing myself upright. Thankfully there was a wall behind for me to lean on. My head hurt like hell. It felt as though someone had implanted an orchestra inside it and they were practising a Beethoven symphony very badly. I tried to shake myself awake and then wished I hadn't as the cymbals clashed between my ears.

My legs were free, which was a blessing, about the only one, unless I counted being alive. I sniffed the air. It smelt of damp and decay and something else that I couldn't quite place. I strained my ears listening for any sound that would give me some indication of where they had brought me. All I could hear was scratching and the light patter of rats.

Slowly my eyes grew accustomed to the dark and I began to identify the smell. The toot of a river barge confirmed it. I was in a derelict building along the Thames somewhere, an old warehouse that hadn't yet been converted into the riverside residence of rich city men and women. I wasn't alone.

In front of me, by the light of a powerful torch, I could see two men standing close to a fallen steel girder. It was Davenham and Motcombe. They weren't arguing exactly but they didn't look like they were discussing the weather either. I guessed they were deciding what to do with me, or rather deciding the best way of disposing of me, as they'd already agreed that I should die.

My eyes searched the dim interior looking for a way out but I couldn't see one. My head was too fuddled to think clearly but unless I did this was it, the end. Davenham glanced my way.

'He's conscious,' I heard him say to Motcombe.

They came towards me. Motcombe was carrying the torch and a gun but it was what was in Davenham's hand that scared me more than either of those items.

'It's all right, Greene, you won't feel a thing. Just a sharp injection and the world will cease to exist for you.'

I ran my tongue around my lips and swallowed. My heart was in overdrive. If it carried on pumping like that they wouldn't need to use the syringe, I'd keel over with a heart attack.

'Then what?' I finally managed to stammer, my voice sounding as though it was coming from a different body.

'The river. When they fish you out it will look like suicide.'

'What's in it?' I jerked my head at the syringe.

'Heroin.'

'Jesus!' I tried to struggle up but Motcombe's hand came down firmly on my shoulder.

'There's no point in struggling. Ben Lydeway did that but it didn't make any difference.'

I slumped. 'You killed him?'

'At first I thought he might come in useful especially when I found out who his sister was and what had happened to her at university. Your file makes very interesting reading, Adam,' Motcombe explained coolly. 'Ben Lydeway believed you'd pushed his sister out of that window and was determined to get his revenge, poor boy. Instead your girlfriend was as high as a kite and probably thought she could fly. Ben had only recently found out what happened to his sister after his mother died and his aunt told him. The family had emigrated to New Zealand shortly after Alison Lydeway's death. It was a bonus that he'd attacked your paintings. I thought the police would charge you but they let you go. It would have been better if they had detained you, that way you might have got to live. Still, the police will make the connection eventually. They'll think you've overdosed, killing yourself because you couldn't live with what you had done, murdering Alison, Ben and Frank Rutland, of course.'

'What motive have I got for killing Rutland?'

'We'll think of one and then plant the evidence. The police won't need much persuading as long as they can tick it off their crime figures. You see there's no way out for you, Adam,' Motcombe said.

But there had to be. Desperately I searched for a solution but my brain had already shut down. Then something totally unexpected happened. I could hardly believe my eyes. I thought I must be imagining it. No, there she was. Jody appeared out of the blackness and she was walking towards us.

'Not giving you any trouble, is he, Pete?'

Motcombe looked surprised for a moment before he smiled. 'He won't get the chance.'

'Good.'

My guts twisted at the scope of her betrayal. I had guessed right, she was in this with Davenham and Motcombe. 'Bitch!' I said fiercely

She stared at me and said, 'Better get it over with.'

But Motcombe was looking puzzled. 'How did you know I was here?'

She dashed a knowing glance at Davenham. Davenham frowned and glanced at Motcombe. I could see that Davenham was ruffled. 'Who the hell is she?' he snarled.

'Oh come on, Tim. The time for pretence is over.' Jody smiled.

'I don't know you,' he spat.

'He's lying of course, Pete.' She addressed Motcombe and moved closer to him. 'Tim has told me all about his laboratory and how he was going to kill you. Yes, you Pete. Why else do you think he insisted on coming here with you? He wanted to make sure you killed Adam Greene and then afterwards he's going to kill you.'

'Rubbish! I never said that. Can't you see what she's trying to do?'

But I could see that Jody had struck a chord. It made a great deal of sense. It didn't take two of them to kill me. Why would Davenham want to soil his hands with murder when he had Motcombe at his beck and call? My brain was beginning to recover.

I said, 'She's right, Motcombe. He can't let you live because you would know too much. Davenham knows that you'll bleed him dry, and make his boyfriend pay too. I see Bransbury's not here to share in the thrills.'

Davenham threw a nervous glance at Motcombe. I pulled at my ropes. I flexed my right hand, trying to ease it out of the loosening bonds. I saw Jody edge towards Motcombe.

Davenham cried, 'You're not going to believe him?'

'Shut up.' Motcombe eased his body round to face Davenham. I was looking at Jody. I saw something that surprised me. Her eyes swivelled towards me and then flicked down at Motcombe's gun. I could no longer tell what were lies and what was the truth but I saw her intention quite clearly. My heart was pumping fast.

I said, 'Maybe there's enough heroin in that syringe for you, Motcombe, as well as me. Did you know that she's Drake's daughter?'

'What!' Motcombe spun back to gaze at Jody. It was enough for Davenham. He plunged the syringe into Motcombe. Motcombe swung back and struck Davenham and the two men fell to the ground as the gun skittered away. Jody dived after it. I struggled against my bonds. The rope gave. I didn't know how long it would be for the drug to take effect, or for one of them to be shot, but I wasn't going to hang around and find out. I glanced at Jody. I didn't know if I could trust her but I had to take a chance. Besides my heart wouldn't let me leave her here.

'Come on.' I finally freed my hand and grabbed Jody's arm. But she shook me off.

'No,' she shouted. 'I've waited a long time for this.' She pointed the gun at Davenham. 'He killed my father and now I'm going to kill him.'

'For Christ's sake, Jody leave it!' But it was too late Davenham lunged out and grabbed Jody's leg. She toppled over and the gun flew from her hand. Davenham reached for it and got it. Motcombe made a grab at Davenham.

I hauled Jody to her feet. 'Run!' I shouted at her. We needed the torch but couldn't waste time trying to find it. She didn't want to run. She wanted to stay. I wrenched at her arm and pulled her away.

As we stumbled away from the sprawling men, I hadn't the faintest idea where I was going and I was dragging an unwilling Jody with me.

'Listen,' I cried breathlessly, spinning her round to face me, as I listened for the sounds of footsteps coming after us. 'Whatever game you're playing it's over. Your father is dead and so is Jack and unless we get out of here *now* we will both be joining them. Is that what you want? Do you want the world to know that your father was a traitor?'

'He wasn't, 'she cried.

'No one will believe that because Davenham will tell it otherwise. Don't you see, Jody; we have to live to tell the truth. Now are you coming?' She nodded. 'This way. I can hear the river. There must be a way out.'

I could feel the cold air on my face and the pungent smell of the river grew stronger. I heard a shot. We froze and looked back but only the black night greeted us.

'Careful,' I cautioned as her foot slipped through a rotting floorboard. 'It looks as though we're on the first or second floor; there are holes all over the place. Take my hand.'

We inched our way across the floor, a stone crashed down through a hole, and we heard it fall against the hard concrete below. Slowly, we edged our way towards the current of air and the smell of the river. At one time there was only a steel girder between us and the floor below. It was like some obstacle in a children's adventure park, I thought, shuffling my feet along it, balancing my body with my arms. But this was no game and there was no soft cushioned special surface to protect us if we fell. I could hear Jody's heavy breathing behind me but couldn't afford to look back at her.

'There's some steps. I don't know how safe they are but we'll have to chance it. We'll have to climb down.' I took her hand, pausing as I thought I heard a noise but I couldn't be sure where it was coming from.

Painfully slowly we climbed down the steps. They seemed sturdy enough; the floor below us though was another matter. What I wouldn't give for a torch. Then as if hearing my plea God lit one; the moon came out from behind the clouds and shone into the building lighting our way. I glanced at Jody who smiled grimly at me. Now we could make better haste. Another flight of steps to the ground floor. Only a few more steps and we'd be by the river and possible escape.

As we raced to the bottom, a figure stepped out. My heart sank. Incredibly it was Davenham. In his left hand he held a cigarette lighter, in his right Motcombe's gun. How the hell had he got here so quickly? Where had he come from? There must have been a quicker, easier way. Jesus, we had gone up and along whilst he'd simply gone along!

'That's far enough,' he commanded.

The flame on the lighter wavered, the moon

went behind a cloud, and without thinking I lunged at Davenham, wrestling him to the ground. The lighter flew from his hand, as I rammed my fist into his face and again.

'Adam, look,' Jody screamed.

I snatched a glance over my shoulder to see orange flames licking up the steps we'd just descended. The wood was rotten and dry; already the space was filling with thick, black acrid smoke, stinging my eyes. I scrambled up and stared down at Davenham.

'No, leave him,' Jody screamed.

I hesitated. 'I can't. He'll burn to death.'

'Adam, you must or we'll be dead.'

She grasped my sleeve. A great crash and the timber fell down inches from me making me leap back. I was coughing. Jody was coughing. At any moment the building would collapse and kill us, or the smoke would get to us. Jack's death would have been for nothing. I had to get out and tell the truth.

'Low. Get down low,' I spluttered. Jody dropped to her knees coughing and choking.

I did the same. 'On your stomach,' I bellowed above the roar of the fire.

The hissing, spitting, crackling fire mocked us,

leaping around us, taunting us: I'll get you yet; you can't escape. We had only seconds to get out. The heat was intense. The smoke terrifying. Then suddenly we were in the fresh air, pressed up against a wall, with a deep, black chasm below us. There was only one way out and that was down. As the flames leapt around us, I screamed, 'Jump, Jody, *jump*.'

I wrapped my arms around her; we teetered on the brink and went over together into the darkness. I just prayed the tide was in or we'd be dead.

The cold water sucked the breath from my body. For a moment I thought my heart had stopped. The water was pulling me under. I thrashed out alarmed. Jody. I had to get to Jody.

With a supreme effort I propelled myself upwards. Then I saw her. The river was alight from the fire behind us and I could hear the sound of the fire engines racing towards it. I cried out and swallowed the foul water. I spluttered and swallowed more. If I survived this I'd probably end up with bubonic plague. Jody swivelled her head. She was treading water.

'I'm all right,' she gasped and began to swim towards me.

Beyond her I could see a riverboat heading for us. It could run us down. I began to wave my arm and call out. Jody did the same.

My body was so heavy. I could barely stay afloat; it was taking every last ounce of energy. I was exhausted. The water was pulling me down. The dirty sludgy river entered my mouth. I spluttered and choked. I couldn't go on. Then I saw Jody; she was struggling. I had to help Jody.

I tried to swim nearer to her but couldn't because of the weight I was carrying. The drone of the boat grew nearer. Jody's head disappeared into the muddy, swirling pool. I had to get to her. I couldn't let her die. I couldn't die now, not when help was so close. It was going to run us down. It wouldn't see us. I raised my hand and shouted. Water entered my mouth. I coughed and spluttered. I felt myself being dragged down. Then hands were hauling me out. Thank God I was safe. But what about Jody? I tried to speak but couldn't. Someone put a blanket around me. Then I heard the words I'd been praying to hear.

'It's all right, mate. We've got her. She's OK.'

CHAPTER 19

It was Christmas Day morning. I stood on the pebbled beach at Hayling and stared across the black velvet sea to the twinkling lights of the Isle of Wight recalling my conversation with a thin, acerbic middle-aged man called Bernard from Special Branch.

After overhearing Davenham's conversation with Bransbury, Bernard had sent Motcombe into Red Watch to discover what Jack was investigating. Then Jack had died and Bernard had enlisted Jody's help to find out if he'd left any notes. Bernard had known that Jody would do anything to find her father's killer. He'd also wanted someone to keep an eye on Motcombe whom he suspected of selling out to Davenham. Someone Motcombe didn't know. He had used Jody just as he had used me. Jody had known nothing about Davenham, or that Motcombe was in Davenham's pay.

But now both Jody and I knew the truth and that the Minister was involved. We could expose the secret.

'Ah, but where's your proof that Bransbury knew about Davenham inappropriately exporting hazardous cargo,' Bernard had said.

'I could make enough noise to make someone take notice, or at least ask some rather pertinent questions. The newspapers perhaps?'

'I don't think that would be wise.'

Or healthy, I thought. 'What about the fire fighters who died from cancer caused by that hazardous waste?'

'Again, where's your proof, Mr Greene?'

With Davenham and Drake dead and the Minister professing ignorance yes, where was my proof? Greys had no record of any fire, there was no fire report, and there was no Rutland or

Honeyman. There was also no computer disk. Bernard's men had searched my boat whilst I was in London and found it.

'And Ian? Jack's colleague? What's happened to him?' I recalled his wife's distraught voice.

'The police are looking for him. He got depressed over his colleague's death. He blames himself.'

'But it was Motcombe who told him to swap.'

'Was it?'

Of course Motcombe wasn't around to confirm it or to tell anyone what he had done with Ian.

When Bernard left I couldn't bear to stay in the same room. The very air was full of his poison. I had been about to leave when Jody had walked in.

'How did you know I was in that warehouse?' I had asked her, still unsure of her.

'Bernard told me.'

'He knew Davenham and Motcombe had taken me there to kill me?' A surge of anger swept through me swiftly followed by a chill that seeped into every bone in my body. It would have been more convenient for Bernard if we had all perished in that blaze, or if the river boat had run Jody and me over in the Thames instead of saving us.

Jody said, 'He told me where I could find my father's killer. I didn't ask questions. I just wanted to find the bastard.'

'You didn't just happen to turn up at the café that morning I found the message in Jack's New Testament and Psalms, did you?'

She shook her head. 'No. I saw you leave Rosie's and then I was told where you were. The personal CD player was a recorder. When I switched it off I was actually switching it over to tape you. When that man threw paint at your pictures, Bernard told me who he was.'

'You knew all about Alison?'

She nodded. Lies. Our whole relationship had been based on lies. I felt anger tinged with bitterness and sorrow. She had deceived me.

Jody said quickly, 'I wanted to tell you but I couldn't. I needed information and you were my best bet of finding it. I'm sorry for deceiving you, Adam, but I had to get to the truth about my father. Don't you see it was all that mattered to me.'

'And now?'

'It still matters but something else does too.'

I wanted to believe her but how could I? 'And the police letting me go after Ben's death? I suppose Special Branch arranged that too?'

'Motcombe had been seen going into the hotel with Ben Lydeway at about the time of the murder. I knew you weren't inside the room because I was speaking to you on the telephone not far from where you were on the beach; I was on the pier.'

'And Simon?'

'You told me where you were going and what you were going to ask him. I called Motcombe and told him. Now I know he called Davenham who telephoned your brother and fed him the information about my father. Motcombe knew where you were.'

'And tried to kill me on Salisbury Plain.' She held my gaze. Had she known that? I thought I saw regret in her eyes but I might have wished it. 'And Motcombe had no idea you were Drake's daughter, hence the false name: Jody Piers.' She nodded.

'I'm sorry you got involved in this, Adam.'

I should have been too but I wasn't. Jack's face swam before me, one moment laughing, his eyes twinkling dangerously, his broad mouth stretched in that cheeky grin, the kind, concerned expression in the pub that night when he'd rescued me from despair; our many sailing trips across to the Isle of Wight, a clear blue sky, a fresh breeze, nothing but the sound of the sea and the wind in the sails. No, I wasn't sorry I'd got involved. In life Jack had given me unconditional friendship, in death he had given me back my self-respect, my strength, myself.

Jody said, 'I had to do it, Adam. You do understand, don't you?'

'I understand,' I said slowly and watched the light come into her eyes. It set my pulse racing. I knew that I cared for her more than I had cared for anyone before, even Alison, but I wasn't sure I trusted her.

She said, 'Do you think there might be a future for us, together?'

'Do you want there to be?'

'Yes.'

I looked steadily at her fighting every instinct and desire in my aching body to enfold her in my arms. 'I need time, Jody.' The disappointment on her face almost made me weaken. I couldn't. I had to think.

I had returned home at the earliest opportunity

packed my bags, collected Boudicca, who didn't seem to mind the move, and gone to live on the boat. On New Year's Day the two of us were going to go sailing for a while. I didn't know exactly where or for how long.

I sniffed the sea air. It felt good. I watched the waves wash on to the shore and out again. The tide was rising just as it always does bringing with it both sorrow and gladness. I heard a fishing boat chugging out to sea. I saw its lights. Time slipped by.

It was over. I'd done what I had set out to do. I'd discovered why those fire fighters had died. I'd completed Jack's mission and I'd found Jack's killers. Perhaps one day I would be able to tell the truth about what had really happened. One day I would expose it. For now I had to remain silent, not for my own sake, that didn't matter to me, but for Rosie. I had to protect her. Jack would have wanted it this way.

I wondered about Bransbury. I guessed that the Prime Minister would be told the facts and that Bransbury would be asked to leave, not only the cabinet, but also politics quicker than you could say by-election. Perhaps Bransbury would be relieved that Davenham had perished in that derelict warehouse; that he would no longer be pulling his strings.

And Jody? Would I ever see her again? I knew I wouldn't forget her and I didn't want to. If she came back into my life I'd be pleased, no, more than that, I'd be complete. Perhaps I would seek her out. I didn't know. Not yet. How could I?

Then there was Faye.

She was oblivious of how my life had changed, ignorant of my brush with death. Even if she knew, or I told her, I could imagine her only half listening before plunging on with her latest new client account. Poor Faye. But that was over. There was no need to pretend anymore, not with Faye, not with Simon, not with Father. And especially there was no need to pretend to myself. I had faced fear and I had conquered it.

In the whispering greyness I watched the dawn arrive reluctantly, almost as if it was afraid of a new day and what it would bring. It licked and sniffed the air not sure about it, a little nervous, a little shocked. I thought of Alison with a calmness that I wouldn't have believed possible before all this. She was the past.

The sun grew in strength; it got brighter and more hopeful until it decided to creep over the edge of the earth. I watched the silvery light in the sky broaden into a pale pink flush in the east and I saw the magic of the sea come alive. In the cold daylight, I had to face the future and I did so with a new but sad heart. I pulled up my collar and started walking.

AN ANDY HORTON MARINE MYSTERY

TIDE OF DEATH

PAULINE ROWSON

TIDE OF DEATH

A MARINE MYSTERY

FEATURING HORTON AND CANTELLI

'Hoist the sails for DI Andy Horton and his sidekick Barney Cantelli. A series with a fair wind behind it and destined to go far.'

Amy Myers

BY THE SAME AUTHOR

It is DI Andy Horton's second day back in Portsmouth CID after being suspended for eight months. Whilst out running in the early morning he trips over the naked battered body of a man on the beach. PC Evans has been stabbed the night before, the DCI is up before a promotion board and Sergeant Cantelli is having trouble with his fifteen-year-old daughter. But Horton's mind is on other things not least of which is trying to prove his innocence after being accused of rape.

Beset by personal problems and aided by Cantelli, Horton sets out to find a killer who will stop at nothing to cover his tracks. As he gets closer to the truth, and his personal investigations start to uncover dark secrets that someone would rather not have exposed, he risks not only his career but also his life…

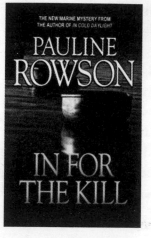

In for the Kill
ISBN 9780955098222
Paperback £6.99

A Gripping Marine Mystery Thriller

Alex Albury has it all: a successful public relations business, a luxurious house, a beautiful wife and two sons. Then one September morning the police burst into his home and arrest him. Now, three and a half years later, newly released from Camp Hill Prison on the Isle of Wight, Alex is intent on finding the man who framed him for fraud and embezzlement. All he knows is his name: James Andover. But who is he? Where is he?

Alex embarks on his quest to track down Andover, but with the trail cold he is frustrated at every turn. Worse, he finds himself under suspicion by the police. The pressure is on and Alex has to unearth the answers and quick. But time is running out. For Alex the future looks bleak and soon he is left with the option – to kill or be killed…

'Packed with twists and turns. Her writing is as sharp as a punch in the ribs. Thoroughly enjoyable.'

Coming soon -

The Suffocating Sea by Pauline Rowson

www.paulinerowson.com

BAJC ARJEN 07|13

This book should be returned/renewed by the latest date shown above. Overdue items incur charges which prevent self-service renewals. Please contact the library.

Wandsworth Libraries
24 hour Renewal Hotline
01159 293388
www.wandsworth.gov.uk

First publi...
MAS...

CONTENTS

Tom   *Joey*

CHAPTER 1

Splat!

Best friends Tom and Joey are spending
their holidays with Joey's parents at
a ski resort. Standing in line on their
skis, the boys wait for a chairlift to take
them to the top of the mountain.

1

Tom "This is the best holiday I've
ever been on in my whole life! Did
I say thanks for inviting me?"

Joey "Yeah, like a million times
already."

Tom "I'm really glad that my folks
gave me enough money to hire
some cool ski gear and take ski
lessons with you. Now I'm like ...
super ski dude."

Joey "I wouldn't say *super*, but you're a heaps better skier than you were five days ago."

Suddenly, two giant snowballs hit the boys—*Splat! Splat!*

Tom "Whoa!"
Joey "Who did that?"

Tom and Joey turn to see three
older boys on snowboards laughing
loudly.

Tom "That sucks! It's those guys
again. They've been throwing
snowballs at everyone all week."

Joey "And now they got us."

Tom "Let's get 'em back."

Joey "Are you nuts? Look how big they are."

Tom and Joey ignore the boys, but within moments they are hit again. *Splat! Splat!*

Tom "Oh, man! That one got me right in the ear."

Joey "Me too. Look! They're heading straight for us."

Tom "We're under attack! What are we gonna do?"

Joey "Quick! Jump on!"

Tom and Joey hurriedly hop onto the chairlift only to discover that the older boys have jumped onto the chair behind them. The chase is on.

CHAPTER 2

On the Run

Sitting on the chairlift, Tom and Joey head for the top of the mountain.

Tom "Are they still there?"

Joey "Um, *yeah!*—where else are they gonna go? They're on a chair, a thousand metres off the ground!"

Tom and Joey look back to see the older boys sneering at them—and still holding some snowballs.

Joey "Right. We're nearly there. When I say go, we've gotta jump off and ski like, a hundred kilometres an hour. If we don't, they'll catch us."

Tom "But I'm still a learner."

Joey "What happened to you being super ski dude?"

Tom "I'm only a super ski dude when I don't have big ski dudes chasing me."

Joey "You'll be alright, just follow me. Ready … go!"

Tom and Joey jump from the chairlift onto the icy slope. Within moments they are flying down the mountain.

Tom and Joey "WHOOOOAAAA!!!!!"

Joey "That's it, Tom! Keep your knees bent and just look straight ahead."

Tom "I am! I am!"

The boys swish past other skiers, darting in and out between them.

Tom (shouting) "There's no way they can catch us now! I wonder if they're behind us?"

Tom looks back.

Joey "Tom, look out!"

Tom turns to see a huge hump directly in front of him. Before he can stop, he skis up and over the hump.

Tom "WHOOOOOOOOAAAAAAAA!!!!!!!!!"

CHAPTER 3

Crocodile Run

Tom flies through the air and crashes back onto the soft, snowy slope with a thud. Joey swishes up beside him.

Joey "Are you okay?"
Tom "Yeah, I think so."

Joey "You were flying! It looked really awesome! Until you landed on your butt and got your skis all tangled up. You sure you're okay?"

Tom "Yeah, I think I can still move my legs and arms."

Joey "Good. Doesn't look like you've broken anything. Now, let's get moving! Those snowball attackers will be here any second."

Tom "But I have to put my skis back on."

Joey "We don't have time for that. Quick, follow me!"

Tom and Joey quickly scramble across the slope into the nearby forest just as the older boys swish by.

Joey "Phew! That was close."

Tom "D'ya think they saw us?"

Joey "No. We got behind these trees just in time."

Tom "Now what?"

Joey "Well, when they get down to the bottom, they'll see that we're not there and they'll probably wait for us to come down."

Tom "Then they'll bomb us with their snowballs."

Joey "Not if I can help it. I've got a plan."

Joey pulls out a folded map from his pocket.

Tom "What's that?"
Joey "It's a map of all the slopes on the mountain. We're on Crocodile Run at the moment."

Tom "Crocodile Run? What a weird name for a ski slope. I'd like to see a crocodile skiing. Maybe it would bite off the arms of the skiers as it went along. That'd be *so* cool!"

Joey "Um, you sure you didn't hit your head when you fell?"

Tom "Never felt better. Now, what's the deal with the map?"

Joey "There's another slope not too far from here. We can get there if we walk through the forest. Then we can ski down it and miss those big dudes completely."

Tom "Cool. Talk about outsmarting 'em. Let's go!"

CHAPTER 4

Freaky Snow Dude

Deep in the forest, Joey and Tom slowly march through the snow.

Tom "I think we should go back. We've been walking for ages. I read back at the resort that skiers shouldn't leave the slopes—ever! It's dangerous."

Joey "Now you tell me!"

Tom "Well, I didn't know you were gonna get us lost, did I?"

Joey "We're not lost."

Tom "No? Then where are we?"

Joey looks around, then back at his map.

Joey "Um, I thought we'd see that other slope by now … um … okay … maybe we're a little bit lost."

Tom "Are you serious? Oh, man, we're gonna die out here. We're gonna freeze to death or get eaten by a pack of wolves."

Joey "There aren't any wolves around here. And we can always build an igloo to keep us warm."

Tom "But what about the abomni ... abomni ..."

Joey "The abominable snowman?"

Tom "Yeah, that freaky snow dude."

Joey "That's just make believe. It's a made-up story."

Tom "No, it's true. I saw it on TV once. It's like this huge half-man, half-ape creature that lives in the forest. And if it finds us, it'll probably pick us up by the feet and have us for dinner."

Suddenly, the sound of a branch snapping echoes from the forest.

Tom "What was that? It's him! The abomni ... aboba ... aboba ... the freaky snow dude!"

Joey "Stop it will ya! Now you're freaking me out!"

Tom "Look!"

A dark figure appears from the trees.

Tom and Joey "ARRRGGGHHH!!!!!!"

CHAPTER 5

Melting Snowmen

As the dark figure draws closer, Tom
and Joey soon realise that it isn't an
abominable snowman, but a ranger.
The boys sigh, relieved to see him.

25

Joey "You should've seen your face. You really thought it was an abominable snowman."

Tom "No, I didn't."

Joey "Yes, you did. You almost peed your pants."

Tom "Yeah, like you didn't."

The ranger tells the boys that they shouldn't have moved off the slopes. He says that Joey's parents were wondering where they were. Luckily, the ranger had been able to follow Tom and Joey's footprints.

Tom "Told you it was a bad idea."
Joey "No, you didn't."

Tom and Joey march a few steps
behind the ranger as he leads them
back down to the resort.

Joey "Well, we're saved anyway …
   but what would you have done
   if it really was an abominable
   snowman? And don't say, run away
   or scream like a girl."

Tom "Yeah, as if! No, I would've got my mum's battery-operated hair dryers out."

Tom grins at Joey.

Joey "Hair dryers?"

Tom "Yeah—one in each hand—and I'd put the settings on really high heat, and blow and melt the freaky snow dude away, until he was just a puddle."

Joey "Yep, I really do think you hit your head when you fell."

The boys make it safely back to the resort and Joey's parents. Their holiday in the snow has come to an end. Joey's parents have packed the car and are ready to leave.

Tom "Hey, look, over there ... it's those guys who threw snowballs at us!"

Joey "Yeah, and they haven't seen us. You thinking what I'm thinking?"

Tom and Joey quickly roll up some snowballs and throw them at the older boys. *Splat! Splat! Splat!* The three boys turn to chase Tom and Joey but it's too late. They've already jumped into the car and are driving off.

Tom "Hey, Joey, have I told you that this is the best holiday I've ever been on in my whole life?"

Tom and Joey laugh. All the older boys can do is stand and watch the car drive away. Tom and Joey wave at them from the back seat.

Snow Lingo

Tom

Joey

abominable snowman A large, hairy creature that lives in the snow. Some people think it's a made-up story and others believe it's real. What do you think?

chairlift A whole lot of chairs hanging from a cable. You sit on one, and it takes you to the top of the mountain.

freaky snow dude An easier way to say abominable snowman—well, at least for Tom it is.

poles The two sticks skiers use to help them keep their balance.

ski run What skiers ski down— sometimes known as a ski slope.

Snow Must-dos

☞ If you want to ski, make sure you have lessons. You especially need to learn how to stop!

☞ When you're out on the ski slopes, watch out for trees. They have a habit of catching you!

☞ Even if you're not a very good skier, you should wear some cool gear and try to look the part.

☞ If you're skiing down a steep hill and you lose your nerve, just sit on your skis and slide down.

☞ If you don't have skis, go sledding or tobogganing instead—it's just as much fun!

☞ If there's plenty of soft snow around, make some snowballs and have a snowball fight with your friends.

☞ If you're going to throw snowballs at older boys, just be sure you can make a quick getaway.

☞ To get into a "snowy mood", watch some snow-themed movies like "Snow Day" or "Snow Dogs", and drink some hot chocolate too!

Snow Instant Info

 Some of the best ski resorts in the world are in the Alps in Europe, Lake Tahoe in America and also in New Zealand. In Australia, the best places for skiing are in the Snowy Mountains in NSW and the Victorian Alps.

 Skis used to be made of wood, but today, most skis are made out of plastic and polyurethane foam.

 One of Australia's most famous ski champions is Winter Olympic gold medallist, Alisa Camplin. She also won a bronze medal in the 2006 Winter Olympics.

Snowboarding developed from skateboarding. Snowboarding became an Olympic sport in 1998.

 The tallest snowman recorded in the Guinness Book of Records was made in Maine, America. The snowman was 34.63 metres tall!

 Everyone knows that some of the Inuits live in igloos made of ice, but did you know that in Jukkasjarvi, Sweden, there's a hotel made out of ice? It's called the Ice Hotel.

 Snow is crystals of frozen water.

BOYZ RULE!
Think Tank

1 What's the one thing you need for a good snowball fight?

2 What's the best way to climb a mountain?

3 What's hot and sweet and best to have after a day of skiing?

4 Do you need ski poles to go snowboarding?

5 Name an Australian ski champion who has the initials "AC".

6 How cold does it have to be for it to snow?

7 What's another name for the abominable snowman?

8 Where's the best place to fall?

Answers

8 The best place to fall is in really soft snow.

7 Another name for the abominable snowman is freaky snow dude.

6 It has to be really, really, really, really cold for it to snow.

5 Alisa Camplin is an Australian ski champion.

4 No, but you do need a snowboard.

3 Hot chocolate is the best thing to have after a day of skiing.

2 The best way to climb a mountain is sitting in a chairlift.

1 For a good snowball fight, you need snow, of course! And other people.

How did you score?

- If you got all 8 answers correct, then go and find yourself a mountain. You were born to have fun in the snow.

- If you got 6 answers correct, then you don't mind a good snowball fight. In fact if it were snowing right now, you wouldn't be reading this—you'd be outside throwing snowballs.

- If you got fewer than 4 answers correct, then you're more of a beach person than a snow dude.

Felice →   ← Phil

Hi Guys!

We have heaps of fun reading and want you to, too. We both believe that being a good reader is really important and so cool.

Try out our suggestions to help you have fun as you read.

At school, why don't you use "Freaky Snow Dude" as a play and you and your friends can be the actors. Set the scene for your play. Bring some ski goggles and ski gloves, or perhaps even skis and poles, to school to use as props. Make some fake snowballs out of rolled-up paper.

So ... have you decided who is going to be Tom and who is going to be Joey? Now, with your friends, read and act out our story in front of the class.

We have a lot of fun when we go to schools and read our stories. After we finish the kids all clap really loudly. When you've finished your play your classmates will do the same. Just remember to look out the window—there might be a talent scout from a television station watching you!

Reading at home is really important and a lot of fun as well.

Take our books home and get someone in your family to read them with you. Maybe they can take on a part in the story.

Remember, reading is a whole lot of fun.

So, as the frog in the local pond would say, Read-it!

And remember, Boyz Rule!

BOYZ RULE!

When We Were Kids

Phil "Do you like snow?"

Felice "I love it. When I was a kid I built this really cool-looking snowman."

Phil "It would be cool … it was made out of snow."

Felice "Ha, ha, very funny. But then this kid came along and kicked it over."

Phil "That's a rotten thing to do. Although, I confess I did that once."

Felice "You did?"

Phil "Yeah, I felt really bad for doing it. It was a really cool-looking snowman with a scarf and a red top hat …"

Felice "… with blue stripes?"

Phil "Yeah … but how did you …? Oops! Sorry."

What a Laugh!

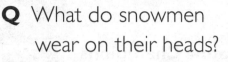

Q What do snowmen wear on their heads?

A Snow caps!

BOYZ RULE!

Read about the fun
that boys have in these
BOYZ RULE! titles:

Pie-eating Champions

Mega Rich

Kite High

Paper Round

Mouse Hunters

Space Invaders

Freaky Snow Dude

Bird Crazy

and more ... !